The Crop of Wickedness

by

H.B. Berlow

The Wichita Chronicles

The Crop of Wickedness

Cover Art by *Tina Lynn Stout*

The Wild Rose Press, Inc.
PO Box 708
Adams Basin, NY 14410-0708
Visit us at www.thewildrosepress.com

Publishing History
First Edition, 2025
Trade Paperback Print ISBN 978-1-5092-6341-7
Digital ISBN 978-1-5092-6342-4

The Wichita Chronicles
Published in the United States of America

Dedication

To Chris Smith (July 17, 1954 - Devember 4, 2024)

He truly had the gift of gab.

Chapter One

Even as I have seen, they that plow iniquity, and sow wickedness, reap the same.
Job 4:8 KJV

It was quite sad to consider I had never been on a picnic before. A thirty-year-old man, a veteran of the Second World War, a former police officer, completely unfamiliar with the rituals of an outing in a park. Vaudeville comedians could easily use the notion as a joke. It had the makings of a character in the Sunday comics. Then again, it certainly wasn't a popular activity for my family in particular or Jewish families in general. The heat, the ants, the pretense of serenity with countless other families milling about. Heck, I didn't even own a short-sleeved shirt which seemed to be the popular wardrobe based on the magazine ads I saw. Eileen Horowitz forgave the slapdash cheese sandwiches, the thermos of room temperature milk, and the macaroons Mrs. Hanover, my landlady, graciously provided me. In the end, my intentions were all that mattered.

A large blanket laid out near Park Villa served as our area of respite. The basket, also borrowed, carried our lunch, such that it was. The sunshine created a warm glow on Eileen's face. Just a week after my belabored attempt at cooking her dinner, we finally realized we had grown from the silly kids in school. I thought there was more in store for us and desperately wanted the relaxation of a warm July afternoon to figure it out, if not make an outright declaration of my possible intentions. At that point, I wasn't sure what they were.

The aimless chitchat was about to segue into a serious conversation when a shiny jet-black limousine rode leisurely down Biting Street. It might have been the low growl of the engine that first caught my attention or the spit shine to it reminiscent of an Army officer's boots. It stopped right across from us and outside of the entrance to Park Villa. It was as though the car itself stared at us. My background and natural inquisitiveness made me concerned it might be associates of Alan Isbell seeking a measure of revenge for their foiled plans.

"You don't see cars like that at the park," Eileen quipped. I agreed.

The man who stepped from the car was close to six feet tall and walked upright, back straight and firm. His uniform was a cross between a standard chauffeur and an English or Australian army man. Highly official with an air of importance. Even with the hat firmly ensconced on his head, I could tell he was bald. His moustache and thick van dyke were black as the car. He exuded far too much formality to be someone intent upon an overthrow of the government, yet just enough malice in his appearance to continue to be concerned.

He looked in both directions before he focused his gaze toward us, then continued forward stoically and with intent. A man of this caliber and in such a vehicle should not have caused any alarm on my part. My inclination dictated otherwise.

He stopped and stood several feet from us, hands at his side, and with no further movement. Initially, he made no effort to speak. I looked over his shoulder.

"Rolls-Royce Phantom?" I inquired.

"Phantom II. Continental." His response carried the slightest touch of pride, closer to respect.

"Would that be a 1931?"

"Thirty-three, sir." The pleasantries did not indicate any concern on his behalf. For the moment. "I'm looking for Mr. Harold Bergman," he continued with an official tone.

"You've found him."

"My name is Liam Smathers. I am in the employ of Mrs. Sylvia Morgan-Smith who requests a consultation with you."

"Great. I can set an appointment for Monday—"

"Now, sir."

It was a definitive statement. Mr. Smathers stopped speaking. He didn't wait for a response so much as an acknowledgement of acquiescence to the request. In that moment, the sun stopped shining on his face and left it in a complete shadow. The darkness of the disagreeable remained.

"I need to escort the young lady home," I finally replied gallantly.

"Miss Horowitz is welcome to join us."

Now I was concerned. The idea that he knew me, looked for me, and then found me could be explained. That was my profession. But he knew the name of my companion, and that presented an otherworldly aspect to it. My car was in the parking lot a good twenty to thirty yards away. To make a run for it didn't make as much sense as acquiescing to a meeting with Mrs. Sylvia Morgan-Smith. The sound of her name carried too much stature to indicate a criminal nature. Then again, neither did "Baby Face" Nelson.

The name rang a bell somehow. It certainly wasn't from any of my social circles, of course. We haphazardly gathered our blanket and basket and followed like good toy soldiers. Eileen and I sat in the back seat, elegantly driven by Liam Smathers in his professional capacity, the full extent of which was still unknown. We traveled east on Eleventh Street and then made a slight turn onto North Emporia where the 1933 Rolls Royce Phantom II Continental pulled into a spacious driveway and toward a mammoth detached garage well in the back. The car stopped just short of it.

The house was mostly brick, two-story, with a large porch, not quite a wraparound. At first, it appeared small in front but it stretched on back to a minimal yard. It was mostly all house, large and boxy, yet with certain flourishes indicative of the Riverside neighborhood. I would have thought someone with the name Sylvia Morgan-Smith would have lived in College Hill or Eastborough, notorious for wealth and elegance. However, after my encounters with Alan Isbell and Albert Whitman, respectively, I was glad to be in one of Wichita's quaint older neighborhoods.

Smathers led the way, opened the front door, and with an extended arm, gestured toward the parlor to our left. Silently, he closed the door behind us and disappeared somewhere within the house. I assumed this was a vague and mysterious way of conducting business, so I went along with it. A woman of this obvious social and financial stature could be allowed her eccentricities. The money implied by the house gave her such authority.

The room was far more elegantly decorated than the prosaic furnishings of the wealthy men I attended to in the last several months. Objets d'art were strewn about, mixed in between the Mission and Victorian furniture. Paintings from the nineteenth century gave the room a museum style quality. The walls were deeply polished mahogany and oak. The furniture plush and elegantly carved. This was the home of someone with rare taste and style, as well as a unique way of hiring a private detective. *It takes all kinds.*

The woman herself sat in a settee that to my untrained eye cost more than the salary of a Captain of Detectives. Her hair was silver with minor flecks of white, coiffured as though we interrupted her attendance at a fundraising event for the Historical Society or the Midtown Horticultural Association. Her black lace dress, however, reeked of mourning. While not as heavy-set as late Queen Victoria, she showed an absolute seriousness to her demeanor. She sat still and composed. With wrinkles around her eyes and mouth, I placed her somewhere in her mid to late sixties.

"I apologize for the melodramatic method of inviting you to my home, Mr. Bergman."

"How may I be of service, Mrs. Morgan-Smith?"

Like Smathers, she referred to the two chairs which matched the settee on the other side of the oak and marble table that separated us like employer and employee.

"I have few pleasures left in my life, Mr. Bergman. Wealth can only mitigate the ravages of age and a life of dissipation."

"And what pleasures give you comfort, ma'am?"

"Companionship, conversation, and discernment."

I nodded empathetically. What came to my mind suddenly came out of my mouth.

"Pleasant words are as an honeycomb, sweet to the soul, and health to the bones."

Eileen smiled in awareness.

Mrs. Morgan-Smith looked uncertain.

"Proverbs 16:24," I answered to the unasked question.

"My understanding is that you are a Jew."

It was phrased as a statement that lacked any degree of judgment. I learned long ago the best course of action in such conversations was to answer directly without a combative quality. Too many people in this world had opinions that bordered on anti-Semitism while others, through their comments, indicated their lack of complete comprehension about the religion or the people.

"I am, ma'am. It gives me comfort and guides me."

She nodded, not as a student of the Bible so much as someone who could perhaps appreciate its teachings. She mentioned a life of dissipation so quickly in passing that I wondered what it might have been. I felt it prudent to defer the inquiry for the moment.

"A gentleman named Arthur Stover had become a trusted friend of mine. We visited, talked of Wichita in the old days. He drank the whiskey and ate the food I offered. He would run errands for me on occasion when Mr. Smathers was preoccupied with his other duties. I came to rely on Mr. Stover for so many things. Now, he has suddenly disappeared. He hasn't been around for nearly two weeks now."

"Did he give any kind of notice?"

She shook her head in disappointment as though I did not fully listen to her dissertation.

"Oh, no, he was not in my employ. Simply a confidant. Someone to share the pleasantries of conversation. As such, I am deeply concerned about his well-being."

I looked toward Eileen. She appeared non-plussed, having never been privy to one of my pre-employment consultations. It was simply second nature for me to turn toward her.

"Do you know where he lives, what he did for a living? Any friends or other acquaintances?"

"Mr. Smathers can provide you with any and all information we have, though I admit it is rather minimal. I hope it will be sufficient enough to aid you on your quest."

To develop a friendship but not know much about the individual sounded rather unusual. She acted like a woman who had lost her cat but her eyes glazed over with desperation. I couldn't tell if she wanted to possess Art Stover or punish him.

"Well, I get twenty-five dollars a day plus expenses. I can certainly provide you with an itemized list—"

She held an envelope thereby cutting off my business spiel in mid-sentence.

"This should cover your efforts. Again, Mr. Smathers will assist you in every fashion possible."

I stood, gave a warm smile, and nodded in acceptance of this case. Eileen paralleled my moves. Last time, when I asked her to accompany me to Alan Isbell's soiree in College Hill it was to be an observer. This time, it seemed she was along for the ride. Although I couldn't be certain how far that would be.

"We'll be in touch," I responded before I realized I implied including Eileen without her permission.

We stepped out of the parlor and stood off to the side. Eileen elbowed me as a way to get me to disclose the contents of the envelope. It was a check for $5000. I couldn't be certain if it represented eagerness or despair. My surprise bordered on concern. I was not that renowned nor dramatically successful in my field enough to warrant such renumeration. There was a part of me almost willing to decline this job. I thought of Proverbs 22:1 – *A good name is rather to be chosen than great riches, and loving favour rather than silver and gold.* Then again, a man has to eat.

An awkward feeling overtook me, one of being watched. I turned and looked down the hall to find Liam Smathers in the doorway to the kitchen. When he saw he gained my attention, he went back into the room. This was what passed for a beckoning gesture. Eileen and I proceeded in that direction.

The kitchen was almost as large as my main living area with perhaps my kitchenette thrown in for good measure. Octagon-and-dot tile on the floor. White subway tile on the walls. Glass-fronted white cabinets. A large white farmhouse sink. An even larger cast iron stove. Above it, an oval from which dangled copper cookware. A rack that held perhaps fifteen knives. A white stoneware container with utensils. Every last nook and cranny clean and spotless. And white. It would appear Mr. Smathers did more than just drive. His culinary skills were yet to be assessed.

I couldn't help but notice my picnic basket on a butcher block table. I hadn't brought it with us initially but figured there were more important questions to be answered.

"What can you tell me about this Art Stover?"

"He was gregarious and rather intelligent on a great many subjects. Politics, history, art. He held his liquor well. Properly dressed but not overly concerned about his wardrobe which was rather out of date. Always respectful of Mrs. Morgan-Smith and never used foul language."

It was a description of character and offered none of the facts necessary to proceed with a search.

"Where did he live?" My tone sounded much like it did when I was a policeman before the war.

"I'm not quite sure."

"Did he have a job?"

"Not that I was aware of."

"Did he mention any family, friends, or acquaintances?"

"None that I can recall."

"What did he and Mrs. Morgan-Smith discuss?"

"I really wasn't privy to their conversations."

It felt like repeatedly lighting a match and blowing it out. This was no way to start a fire.

"Mr. Smathers, you realize your employer has asked me to locate Art Stover. She led me to believe you would have substantial enough information for me to initiate this task. With what you've told me, I couldn't find him if he was standing in front of me."

Eileen tugged on the back of my jacket. It was her way to let me know she thought I acted disagreeably. She hadn't fully grasped what it took to do this job. Maybe her way was better after all.

"My apologies, Mr. Bergman. Perhaps I do have some bits of information. But, in truth, I think this pursuit is a fool's paradise."

Given his stalwart appearance and sense of loyalty, this kind of honesty took me aback. It was one thing to disagree with a moneyed employer but a whole other matter to verbalize it.

"Why is that, Mr. Smathers?"

"From what I gathered, Mr. Stover discussed a wide variety of subjects with Mrs. Morgan-Smith. Interior decorating. The Stock Market. Landscaping. Law enforcement. Automotive mechanics. It led me to believe he saw being in her employ full-time as a lucrative opportunity."

"And the possibility of your dismissal."

"Yes, sir. Assisting you with finding Mr. Stover would be akin to—"

I couldn't tell if he was thinking of the proper example or afraid to declare it.

"What exactly?"

"Carrying my own cross."

The fee I received was far too great to make moral judgments with regard to the propriety involved with Liam Smathers' employment. It would be significantly more difficult to begin this process without some small bits of information. By the same token, I didn't want this hulking man to become an adversary right from the start. I made a concession to advise him of my progress which he could relate to our mutual employer. In return, he "assured me he would pass along any recollections or bits of information that might be useful in this endeavor.

From that brief agreement, I got a general description, an address, a car make and model, and two names, one that I recognized as a police officer. Since I was ready to leave, I requested to be driven to Park Villa. Instead, Liam Smathers brought Eileen and I to the door where my car was parked in front. I was perplexed. He handed the picnic basket to Eileen, and we left the house. Once inside, a pleasant aroma overtook us. Inside the basket were two roast beef sandwiches, a small jar of dill pickles, and two ripe peaches.

I realized it might be prudent to have Liam Smathers cater my next picnic.

Chapter Two

The aroma of roast beef wafted around my car to the extent it made me wonder what I actually ate for the past several years. There were no concerns as to whether or not it was kosher. If Mrs. Morgan-Smith was aware of my religion, her manservant likely considered my culinary preferences. It started off as the most unique job I was hired to do. My mind cleared from distraction when Eileen finally spoke.

"Well, where do we start?"

I looked at her askance, and wondered if her inquiry was lighthearted or serious. Her eager smile led me to believe the latter.

"This is Wichita, not Hollywood. I am not William Powell. You are not Myrna Loy. And unless I'm mistaken, neither Lady Mittens or Sir Pounce could pass for a wire-haired fox terrier."

"I know we're not Nick and Nora," she started apologetically before I cut her off.

"Eileen, this is not fun and games. This is serious stuff. It's very easy to get hurt. Have you forgotten Alan Isbell and Zack Molloy?"

"I know."

"You've got a rich gal wanting to find her 'companion' and a thug who thinks he's a majordomo not wanting this guy to be found. And after my last couple of cases and rummaging around Eastborough and

College Hill, I am really starting to distrust these rich folks."

"But they do pay well."

On that point, she received no retort. It was also difficult to reconcile the notion of making a substantial living while being employed by people with questionable morals. Those tough guy detectives of the movies were not as conflicted as I became. We continued on in silence until we got to her apartment. I debated whether to be tough or tender. I didn't get a chance as she spoke first.

"The only excitement in my life is the tidbits I get working the switchboard at the *Beacon.* Eventually, I will settle into the life of a homemaker, wife, and mother. I just want to live a little before then. Is that such a bad thing?"

When I considered my job as a police officer, my life as a soldier, and my recent profession as a private detective, I knew more excitement than most people experienced. It wasn't, however, all thrills. I put my life in the crosshairs to find someone's daughter or husband. That meant I allowed myself to be the target to save someone in jeopardy. It was a way of determining who I really was and what I was ultimately capable of doing. I understood what Eileen wanted, now and later. This was not it.

I offered her the contents of the picnic basket. She reminded me of my limited culinary skills and advised I should take it. Our kiss was one of temporary goodbye. I put her aside for the time but knowing her as I did, she would certainly press the matter.

A quick stop by the main police station was worth the possibility of any indirect information about Art

Stover. Melvin Bronsky held down the fort. He enjoyed the extra shifts as a desk sergeant because of his five children. First, he made more money. Second, he was glad to be away from his five children. He always looked as though he had not gotten enough sleep. Both his work and his family led him to that appearance.

"Mel, what do you know about Art Stover?"

"Name rings a bell," he replied while he looked at the ceiling to jog his memory. "Private dick, I think. Like you."

That surprised me. I tried to imagine such a decline in my business that I needed to take on the chores of companion to an elderly rich woman. Then again, he might have been more like the late Mickey Dowell. Anything for a buck as long as it was relatively legal and not subject to too much scrutiny.

"Any gab on him?"

"Nothing to speak of." Just then, Detective H.L. Watts of the Night Detective Squad, walked past with a handful of files, a sharpened pencil stuck behind his ear. "Watts, Bergman here is looking for scoop on Art Stover."

I never met H.L. Watts before, only knew him by reputation through my buddy Clarence Mendenhall, the head of the squad. Apparently, Watts was the final selection after many desperate attempts to lure me back after the war. Anyone invited to join had to have immaculate qualifications so I couldn't doubt his skills.

"Hey, Bergman." We shook hands. "Stover, huh? Doesn't beat on our door all that often. Only thing I can recall is him nosing around a couple of months ago about the killing of Chubb McFarland."

"That the old timey bootlegger?"

"One and the same."

"What was Stover's interest in him?"

"Couldn't tell you."

Watts indicated a backlog of reports, so I let him go on his way.

I knew there had to be other facts about McFarland that I couldn't remember. As best as I could figure, he would be about the same age as my client. Perhaps Art Stover had been hired to solve his murder. Then again, what would a highfalutin wealthy matron have to do with a rumrunner from the 1920s? I'm sure she had the means in those days to have a well-stocked liquor cabinet without associating with the hoi polloi. Most of those types did. On occasion, the thrill of rubbing elbows with 'bad men' got the better of these folks. Mrs. Sylvia Morgan-Smith did not come across as a thrill seeker.

"Mel, if you get a chance can you check out a Liam Smathers and see if he has a record?"

"For what?"

"Anything."

Though this wasn't official police business, Melvin relished the opportunity to keep busy. I did what little research I could at the police station. I checked the clock in the main foyer and saw I had a scant forty-five minutes before the Carnegie Library closed. My real research would start now.

Karla Duggan was somewhere in her forties with vibrant red hair. She had the gamin-like quality of Tinkerbell with the spicy retorts of Martha Raye. What really fascinated most people was a mind that absorbed knowledge and information like a sot drinks cheap hooch. Once she read a book or newspaper or magazine, it was imbedded in her mind. She could put the Dewey

Decimal system to shame. In that regard, she was more than qualified to be the facility's principal research librarian and my greatest source of information. That made it easier for me to stay away from bums and derelicts scrounging for some loose change.

"I would have expected to find you under a chuppah by now," she said immediately upon seeing me.

"To every thing there is a season, and a time to every purpose under the heaven."

"Yep. Good old Ecclesiastes. I stepped right into that one. You would have made a great rabbi. Or so I have been told."

We both smiled. I had too much respect for her to merely walk in and question her like it was an interrogation. In return, her quips about my life were expelled like vaudeville jokes.

"I've got some names to throw at you. You mind?"

"Shoot."

"Art Stover?"

"Small fry. Not anywhere as good as you."

"Private?"

"Yep. I can't recall too many clippings regarding his successes. More the kind to scrape by on the q.t."

"When has he been in the papers?"

"Mostly arrests on trespassing or disturbing the public peace. All in the course of his so-called profession."

"Fair enough. Liam Smathers?" She shook her head negatively. "He works for Sylvia Morgan-Smith."

"Rich dame but not high society."

"What do you mean by that?"

"Big house. Big car. A few mentions in big circles. Seems to play it close to the vest."

When I thought about Albert Whitman and Alan Isbell, it occurred to me those with money kept a lower profile to avoid any undue entanglements. It didn't mean they were successful.

"Last one. George McFarland?"

"Chubb."

She blurted it like she referenced an old friend.

"Okay, spill."

"You know how I am fascinated by the criminal element in this city. Even as far back as Wyatt Earp."

I merely stared at her in an attempt to get her to continue.

"He was killed recently."

"Yes, I was just made aware of that. So?"

"He ran around with Eddie Adams."

That was the missing something. Eddie Adams started as a two-bit punk. However, in a little over twelve months in the early 1920s, he went on a crime spree in which he killed seven people, that included three police officers, wounded several dozen more, and netted over $45,000 in late 1921. A police officer killed him right here in Wichita the day before Thanksgiving that year.

Maybe Art Stover's interest in this bootlegger's killing had nothing to do with Mrs. Morgan-Smith. Until I was able to discern a reason for this curiosity, I could not even attempt to locate Stover. Liam Smathers indicated he believed Stover lived in the Shirkmere Apartments over on Topeka and Second Street. I found a listing for him in the Polk directory that indicated a flophouse over on Wabash south of Thirteenth. That was either Smathers being wrong or deceitful. Either one was a distinct possibility.

The front desk clerk at the Shirkmere was a skinny,

balding officious man whose cologne reeked of hyacinth. He was familiar with Art Stover, mentioned encountering him on several occasions while he visited what he assumed were friends, but assured me in no uncertain terms that Art Stover did not live there. Now or prior. Additionally, there were no specific names of people he may have claimed to visit. The self-satisfied gentlemen determined he had been accommodating despite my belief to the contrary. I assumed Stover greased him in the past for information or privacy. The fact I was disinclined to be as obliging ended the interview.

I encountered no such formality at the location further north. A row of four brick apartments appeared like a small factory abandoned after a bombing. It brought back hideous memories of unfortunate civilians who were caught in a game they didn't choose to play. A wooden railing at the curb, similar to where a cowboy might park his horse, held four rusted mailboxes. The box for unit number three had the name STOVER in paper that yellowed considerably. The door was unlocked.

As simple as Arlene Nathan's home was, this was a shack by comparison. It was one room with a bed, a chair, a kitchen table, a counter with a small sink and a hot-plate to the side, a two-drawer dresser, and a water-closet with a shower so narrow it looked more like a coffin. It didn't even have a window to look outside. The room smelled of mildew and burned meat. A threadbare blanket covered the bed. A dirty dish and fork sat in the sink. I rummaged through the dresser and found several shirts, a pair of pants, three pairs of underwear and three pairs of black socks, and two garish ties. I reached underneath each drawer for any item that might have been taped for security. Nothing. For a man who spent several months serving as a companion to an exceedingly wealthy woman, I saw no visible evidence of gratuity or generosity as compensation. A shaving mug and comb sat on the sink by the shower.

As I turned toward the room, a small item caught my eye at the bed. It was a paper of some sort sticking out from the pillow case. When I approached, it became evident it was part of a newspaper. Using only fingertips, I removed it from its place of comfort and held it in such a way as to peruse what might have been important to Art Stover.

It was a page from the *Beacon* dated Friday June 21. The article described the death of George McFarland, known by many in underworld circles as Chubb. He was found stabbed in an alley not far from the Orpheum Theater, the apparent victim of a robbery. His inner pockets were rifled and there was no wallet. He was identified by retired patrolman Abraham Meyer who was on the force when Eddie Adams was killed. McFarland's incarceration on charges unrelated to his association with Adams was mentioned. His dealings and whereabouts of the past several years after his parole were unknown. The tone of the article indicated the police continued their investigation though not as vigorously given the nature of the victim. Just another exclamation point to a long-ago piece of history.

By the time I got on the police force in 1937, Eddie Adams was old news. A few of the veterans had stories they would share if you lent them your ear. For the most part, nobody wanted to discuss a gonif who thought he was a button man, especially one who had no second thoughts about killing policemen. Even Abe Meyer, who retired shortly thereafter, didn't think Eddie Adams and his crowd were worth a second word. Just a dark piece of the past that most wanted to forget. So, why did Art Stover have such an interest in him?

It is likely I would need to stop by the station and talk with Clarence Mendenhall of the Night Detective Squad to see if the Records Room had old files on Adams. That night in November of 1921 and the recent death of Chubb McFarland got Art Stover's dander up. With twenty-five years gone by, I couldn't imagine what it might be.

Chapter Three

In my four years on the Wichita Police Department, I had made quite a few friends, largely due to the fact I was deferential and treated most with respect. With the exception of Marty Hoeg who was as corrupt as the day is long, I questioned and learned everything I could. It was likely I would have been promoted to detective were it not for Pearl Harbor. My enlistment was my own choice, and I had no regrets fighting for my country.

I built enough consideration that, even now as a private detective, it was easy to ask questions and get viable answers as long as it didn't involve an active case. I fully understood the propriety of it as I did when I was on the force myself. That was where I got most of my current information when it didn't come from Karla Duggan.

I was surprised to see Lt. Raymond Anderson in the records room on a Sunday morning. He wasn't in uniform, instead appeared more like a businessman with suit jacket and tie. He had a stack of files before him, as one hand rubbed his forehead, and the other hand held a cigarette from which he puffed madly. He paid little attention while ash continued to grow like Pinocchio's nose. A combination of desperation, frustration, and fatigue can do strange things to a policeman.

"Bim", as he was called, looked like he had a perpetual tan. An Arizona native, he was tall and outdoorsy, a less-cowboy version of Gary Cooper with an equally laid-back attitude but a determined approach to just about everything. Except when he ran against a wall. I stood in silence until he finally looked up and smiled.

"Bergman," he uttered. "Visiting old ghosts?"

"With your help, yes."

I caught him off guard with the comment and then explained I needed info on Eddie Adams.

Without so much as a pause, he rattled off everything that was in the files on the desperado who crammed a criminal career into a brief fourteen months, which was slightly longer than John Dillinger twelve years later. But Adams didn't have the same panache or style as Dillinger. Didn't have the John Gilbert moustache and smile. Or maybe he didn't have a press secretary.

Lt. Bim Anderson recited all the facts as though it were a doctoral thesis:

Daylight robbery of a Kansas City gambling den, September 5, 1920. Sentenced to life in prison, February, 1921. While transported to prison, jumped off a train to escape, then joined in the robbery of a bank and general store, February 11, 1921. Captured and sent to prison. Escaped again in August, 1921. Further robberies, shootouts, and killings in September and October until he was shot to death by Officer D.C. Stuckey in a Wichita garage, but only after Adams killed Detective Charles Hoffman and Officer Charles Bowman. If Wichita had a museum dedicated to its criminal history, Lt. Anderson would have been a prime candidate as a docent.

"Okay, so this was before you and me," he

continued in a more casual fashion. “You writing a book? Or is there something else that tickled your fancy on this thug? This is twenty-five years ago, Harold. There’s a lot of dust on that shelf.”

“Chubb McFarland died recently,” I stated as simply as possible.

“Yep.”

“Any word on that?” Bim shrugged his shoulders. “Paper said it was a robbery.”

“Could have been.” Lt. Anderson acted as professional as possible while at the same time he tried to assist me with an as-yet-unknown inquiry. “You know what’s even more interesting than McFarland’s death? Nellie Miles was found dead near Park Villa last fall.”

It was my turn to shrug. Bim identified the victim as a former local madam and long-time friend of Eddie Adams. The night before Adams’ demise, two carloads of rabble rousers were pulled over by two motorcycle policemen. A shot was fired that killed patrolmen Robert Fitzpatrick. All the women there that evening were released later while the men fled south to somewhere in Cowley County. Perhaps it was just a coincidence but two people associated with Eddie Adams were killed within the last nine months. This was nearly a quarter century after the incidents described. It was when I asked Bim if he knew of any other deaths of known associates, he finally went to the file cabinets.

“Kansas City police reported the death of a P.D. Orcutt on August 11, 1945, two days after the bombing of Nagasaki. Says here his neck had been broken. But there was no indication of robbery. He was in the vicinity of a known opium den. Other than that, no further leads. They deactivated the case but as you know, they never close it." He put the file down and just looked at me in expectation of a response. I had none.

A pattern of a sort emerged. What perplexed me was how Art Stover got involved. Perhaps his discussions with Mrs. Morgan-Smith led to some revelation that caught Stover's attention. That seemed impossible as the lady was upper crust in all things. She couldn't possibly have known anyone connected with crimes from that time period. Her chauffeur, on the other hand, was a different story all together.

"You got a file on a Liam Smathers?" I said as I turned from the doorway.

"Officially, a few traffic tickets. Likes to drive that fancy car a little too fast at times."

"How about unofficially?"

He walked toward me as though to prevent anyone from eavesdropping.

"He has all the marks of an ex-con though we don't have a file on him. If you met him, you know what I mean. This isn't much but there are rumors he was a mercenary for the IRA in '22 and for Abd el-Krim in the Rif War in '23."

"I can see it. So, I wonder if he was anywhere near Kansas City in 1945."

"Why don't you ask him?"

Bim's punchline fell flat.

The closest people I knew who mingled in high society were Bradley Wolrebinski and his wife, Svetlana Halonen. Bradley wrote lurid pulp novels under the name R.C. Donnelly while Svetlana was a painter of some note. They lived in a huge Victorian house on Park Place where Svetlana turned her artistic talents on the landscaping. I bonded with them over the years because they were gregarious, welcoming, and Jewish. I never knew for certain how they earned their income. I never asked. The air of mystery maintained an allure to our friendship.

It was early Sunday afternoon so I figured they would be recovered from whatever late-night soiree they had attended. I learned otherwise as my gentle knock on their massive oak front door yielded a heavy-set man who appeared afraid of the sunshine. He pulled me in and shut the door behind us in a brave attempt to dispel the offending light.

"Happy Bastille Day!" I declared with enthusiasm. I hoped to get Bradley to talk about French peasants or cuisine. He did neither.

Instead, he walked in a plodding fashion toward the parlor, a room I became intimately familiar with through the years. Conversations, chess, and schnapps were shared in this room. The artistic sensibilities of my two dear friends balanced the logical police mentality and the deep concern associated with a man whose father would have preferred him to be a rabbi. These two were about as real as the sun and the sky and the moon.

"We celebrated last night. Several magnums of champagne. The French know their bubbles." As though finally sobering up, he looked at me with great eagerness. "What brings you out today? Certainly not any Gallic conversation."

"Mrs. Sylvia Morgan-Smith."

He nodded knowingly.

"She's my client."

He beamed regally.

"A highly lucrative scenario. You could retire working for her. In any fashion."

"Rich?"

"Is the Pope Catholic?"

"What's her background?"

Here was the familiar pattern. I could ask Bradley a question, some inquiry that was entirely within his purview. Yet he would dwell on it for a moment, as though trying to find, as Flaubert indicated, *le mot juste,* the right word. I knew too few writers but imagined them to be all the same.

"We met her at a fundraising event at the Innes Tea Room in, um, 1931."

"1932," Svetlana shouted from somewhere in another room. She waltzed into the parlor draped in a *shmatte* that resembled an apron. She wore gloves and held pruning shears. A bit of dirt was on her nose. I wondered if she heard us from her garden. I wouldn't put it past her.

"She's probably right," Bradley acquiesced with a bit of a shrug.

"The woman is a pig." The comment caught me off guard, but I knew not to interject as there was likely more to be said. "She tries to buy class but has none. Moved here from Kansas City after her husband died, or at least that was what she said. *Pishtosh.* She said a lot of things that were *drek.* After a few attempts to ingratiate herself into the art community, she basically insulated herself inside that monstrosity of a house with a block of quartz that looks like Kemal Ataturk."

Mrs. Morgan-Smith's house, in my modest opinion, was beautifully designed and meticulously decorated, appealing rather than ornate, likely given the lack of social events that occurred there. And, while Liam Smathers lacked any discernible charm, he presented himself as devoted to his employer. I knew Svetlana had higher standards and passed off the comments as opinion more than fact. What I really wanted to know about was her life in Kansas City. Bradley and Svetlana looked at each other perplexed. Bradley finally shrugged.

"Beyond those early days, we have had no major contact with her. She never became part of our circle." I obviously appeared dismayed, and Bradley seemed confused by it. "If she's your client, why don't you ask her?"

"It's far too delicate of a matter. Besides, you don't ask a wealthy client if she ever knew Eddie Adams."

It was this that caught Bradley's attention. Crime fiction was his genre. True crime was his hobby, a passion and an avocation rolled into one. In the past, he provided comments and speculations that, to a former policeman, might only have come from someone with intimate knowledge of such activities. Then as now, Bradley was never implicated in any act deemed illegal by the state of Kansas. For lack of that, insinuation took its place. I took his advice for what it was worth.

Now, however, I found myself questioning the motivations of a client based on innuendo and scant speculation. The man she hired me to locate was the one interested in associates of a criminal dead now for twenty-five years. I found no reason to believe or assume she had any connection with that criminal. No discernible facts to tie her to a brigand. The case with Albert Whitman spoiled me, turned my already stubborn thoughts about the wealthy into a comprehensive distaste. I stopped, breathed, and reminded myself of a passage from Berachot 58a in the Talmud – *No two minds are alike just as no two faces are alike.*

"Do you know anyone who knows her well? Is it possible someone could be that wealthy with virtual no social connections?"

Bradley was non-plussed. Svetlana lifted her head as though she sought wisdom from Adonai. It must have come.

"Arch Butts," she said plainly.

"The Packard dealer?"

"Yes. I recall there was some cocktail party, many moons ago. This Morgan-Smith woman sought a chauffeur. Well, first, she needed a car. Naturally, Arch inserted himself into the conversation and indicated he could help her with both." She paused, then suddenly declared, "My roses need pruning," turned and left. I took it that meant she had nothing further to add to the conversation.

Bradley had the option of inviting me for a game of chess and a mid-afternoon aperitif or shrugging his shoulders and admitting he was out of ideas as well. He chose the latter.

A quick stop at Zongker Drugs on North Waco not far from Bradley and Svetlana's house provided me with a phone booth and the Polk directory. Jacob Archibald Butts lived at 290 South Pershing, right on the edge of College Hill where the fabulously wealthy people most typically resided. This one might prove beneficial to my needs.

My foot throbbed, not from any extensive walking but likely from my attitude. I wondered whether my subtle contempt of the upper classes was due to any kind of jealousy. As is said in Proverbs 14:30 – *A sound heart is the life of the flesh: but envy the rottenness of the bones.* It wasn't envy but a bullet and shrapnel tearing into my foot and ankle that caused it to weaken. No amount of money would restore my balance or provide any greater degree of comfort. Additionally, I knew too well that not all those who were well off were unscrupulous. Unfortunately, just those I encountered thus far.

By the time I turned onto South Pershing from Douglas Avenue, it occurred to me I didn't have any reason for making inquiries of a successful businessman I didn't even know. On a Sunday, no less. I had to determine whether to use the official tone of a police officer, the respectful voice of a military man, or the compassionate demeanor of a man of the cloth. There was no time to decide as the door opened quickly after the first knock.

The gentleman was in his late sixties, gray hair overtaking most of the deep black, extremely serious eyes behind round wire-rimmed glasses, and a look of stoic immutability. He could have been a professor or an accountant. I could not, however, determine his attitude merely from his appearance.

"Mr. Butts, my name is Harold Bergman," I began before he interrupted.

"Bergman? Your father the watch repair man?"

"Yes, sir."

A soft smile appeared briefly.

"Good man."

My father's reputation preceded him and, in this case, opened a door. Unfortunately, not wide enough for an invitation to enter. Consequently, I needed to be direct and brief.

"I understand you sold Mrs. Sylvia Morgan-Smith a car some years ago."

"Packard 840 Deluxe. Brand new." He rattled off the description without a second thought. What secretary could be as efficient?

"Did you also recommend Liam Smathers to her as a chauffeur?"

"Never heard of him." His bluntness caught me off guard. "We had an employee by the name of William Fintelman who was about to be fired. I did the Christian thing and referred him to Mrs. Morgan-Smith."

"Interesting."

"Why is that?"

"I was under the impression Smathers was with her when she moved from Kansas City."

"Wouldn't know a thing about that. I do know she went and bought a Rolls Royce a couple of years later. Never did business with her again."

"Perfectly understandable."

I knew it wouldn't be prudent to press Mr. Butts for more information so I thanked him for his time and apologized for any inconvenience. Strangely, he never asked me the reason for the inquiry. Brevity is not only the soul of wit but a benefit to the inquisitive.

While there were numerous inquiries, nothing that I did this day got me any closer to finding Art Stover or learn anything further about him which was the primary reason I was hired. This was a fact as stated by a former policeman. What I did get was a thread, a name, someone who might be connected to both Stover and the lady with whom he shared many confidences and secrets. It was time to pry them apart.

Chapter Four

It had been a while since I visited my father. With his reputation foremost in my mind after the encounter with Butts, I found myself in good spirits enough to invite my father to dinner. His house on South Kansas Street, the house I grew up in, was close to his watch repair and jewelry shop and very close to the temple. My father needed to be close to his abode, his synagogue, and his place of business. This kind of proximity grounded him as well as made him realize they were equally important at this point in his life. I hoped to find that same balance.

The aroma from inside made me realize he already prepared dinner. His smile was the only invitation I required along with a knowing look on his face when I told him why I was there.

"I have a chicken in the oven and some boiled potatoes on the stove. They should be ready in about five minutes." Could it be my father was a seer, the prophet that came after Malachi? Or had I simply given my father ethereal qualities over and above his simple earthly means? I tossed some greens together with olive oil, salt and pepper, while he carved the chicken and scooped the potatoes on a plate. I wore the yarmulke he always made available for me at the front door, and we bowed our heads in prayer.

"*Barukh ata Adonai Eloheinu, Melekh ha'olam,*

bo're minei m'zonot," my father intoned.

"Blessed are you, Lord our God, King of the universe, Who creates all manner of nourishment," I replied.

"Amen."

"Amen."

As was typical from the days of my youth, we ate in silence. Any repast was supposed to be consumed with the proper respect it deserved. Only after our plates were cleaned did we look up and smile in satisfaction. My father put the leftover chicken and potatoes away while I cleaned the dishes. Then, in keeping with our traditions as adults, we sat in the parlor, my father smoked his pipe, and we talked. It was natural for him to ask what case I was involved with at the time. Though he would have preferred me to be a rabbi, he took a respectful interest in my career choice. It gave him further insight into his own son.

"I hear in your description of this woman," he started after a moment of reflection, "the same type of bitterness with regard to that man in Eastborough."

"I have no bitterness toward Mrs. Morgan-Smith."

My father had a habit of using his pipe for emphasis when I exhibited a youthful stubbornness. Though I recently turned thirty, I was still my father's son, perhaps more willful than I intended to be and still deserved to be admonished on occasion.

"She hires you to find someone, and you spend your time trying to learn about her, perhaps discover her follies."

"Sometimes it's necessary to know who is seeking in order to determine who is being sought."

My dad shrugged his shoulders at me in place of a

verbal disagreement. It was his way of getting me to elaborate, especially if he recognized I had a smattering of logic in my actions.

"If this lady has good intentions, why has the man disappeared? If her desire is based in something nefarious, I will need to look for this man in hidden places."

He waved me off with his pipe before he refilled and lit it again. Though he listened, it was clear he disagreed.

"You focus too much on intention and desire and less on seeking directly for this man. Think about your own intentions."

I understood my father did not desire to be harsh with me, but his comments contained a kernel of truth to them.

"Of late, you have been hired by people of means whose repute you question. Then why work for them? To cast aspersions at them is no different than those who believe Jews have horns and were the killers of Christ. We must maintain our integrity and remain firmly rooted in the world. As it is and as Adonai intended."

That feeling of being lost came over me again. This time it was my own doing. I recalled from Pirkei Avot 4:21 – *Rabbi Elazar ha-kappar said: envy, lust, and vainglory put a man out of the world.* I realized I sought enemies long before I could recognize friends. This was not the manner in which I intended to live. My client needed only to find a man she came to rely on. One simple task. My judgment in this matter was not necessary nor required to complete it.

My father did not know of police work, what it took to be a soldier in a theater of war, or the trade of a private investigator. He knew humanity. He understood the world in a way the deepest philosophers could not grasp. He was, more than anything else, a devoted Jew who gave thanks to the Almighty for the blessings of simply being alive and given the opportunity to worship. It would have been pleasing to me to feel the same way. Perhaps the things I experienced would eventually bring me to the same place but in a more circuitous fashion, one that I could not as yet identify. I could only hope this was so.

I felt like having dessert but opted not to go someplace like Candyland or Ciro's. Because Eileen was not fond of the Pan American Restaurant, I hadn't spent as much time there of late. King Mar, the jovial and gregarious owner, built quite a business and reputation since emigrating from China over twenty years prior. I felt comfortable around him and was grateful for his generosity.

A big hug nearly squeezed the life out of me. He indicated his chef tried to make a Boston cream pie and offered me a piece to get my opinion. After he described the moist vanilla cake, custard, and chocolate fondant, I was seduced into acceptance. He started to walk away and then turned suddenly.

"There's a guy who's been looking—" he began just as I asked "—Have you ever heard of a guy named Art Stover?"

"That's the guy," he bellowed, much to the chagrin of the few remaining customers.

"What guy?"

"The guy who's been looking for you."

"Art Stover?"

"Yes."

King Mar indicated Stover had stopped by that

morning, shortly after the restaurant opened. He asked for me by name, seemingly aware of my tendency to frequent the place. Stover acted calm but somewhat desperate, according to King Mar. When Stover left the restaurant, he waited in the doorway, looked up and down the street for quite some time before he departed on foot.

"How did he leave it?" I asked, as though this were one of Bradley Wolrebinski's novels.

"Green Gables. Tonight. Midnight. It was funny though."

"What was?"

"He seemed to know I would see you before then."

A juke joint and cheap roadhouse on Thirteenth Street well outside of city limits, Green Gables was owned and operated by Glick Helbert and a couple of other nasty characters. My dealings with Helbert and his associates went back to when I tangled with corrupt cop Marty Hoeg. I scared Glick enough to put the actual bad guys away, but I was pretty sure his chest puffed back out after all of that cleared. I wasn't concerned because I had no interest in pursuing him to clean up the city and eliminate vice. I left that job to the real police.

I had no other choice. My client tasked me with locating Art Stover. As it turned out, Art Stover sought me. This was an invitation I was required to accept, professionally speaking. At this point, however, it was nearly eight o'clock. I was no longer a policeman on a late shift or an infantryman up all night to guard a post. For nearly a year, I had been a civilian who made my own hours and got to bed at a typically decent hour of the night.

I drove home and fed the cats which did not take as

much time as I would have liked. Lady Mittens sat comfortably next to me on my love seat while Sir Pounce lay at my feet and rolled in comfort at the fullness of his belly. They would likely be on my bed by the time this late-night adventure was concluded. Whenever that turned out to be.

There was never a thought as to what would happen if I didn't return home. Just as Mrs. Hanover, my landlady, was able to convince me to accept the responsibility of feline maintenance, someone of an equal heart would do the same. My thoughts turned to Eileen. We had gotten considerably closer over the last several weeks. A vague notion of sustaining this relationship, perhaps expanding upon it to its natural end lingered in my mind. It was then I tried to consider what it would be like to go for a midnight meeting on some case and what that would do to her. I thought about it until it was time to go. It sickened me to imagine it. And then I couldn't think of it any longer.

Even though it was a pleasantly warm summer night, these kinds of establishments typically didn't attract large crowds on Sundays. That was only an impression and not a declaration based on experience. As I approached, I saw a handful of cars on the dirt patch that passed for a parking lot. Based on the way Stover approached King Mar, I figured this to be a meeting on the q.t. so it was best to park at a distance from the entrance. A whispered voice called to me no sooner than I emerged from the car.

"Bergman?"

I stood still and didn't reply. Of course, I figured it to be Stover, but this was his show, and I let him direct the traffic.

I turned my head in the direction of the voice. The night air played tricks with me. As I turned around, Art Stover was right by my side. He was slightly shorter than me with a beard like sandpaper. His hair was a mix of salt and pepper as they say. I guessed him to be in his mid-fifties, perhaps even over sixty. His eyes looked withered as though he hadn't slept in a while and not of his own choice. I finally recognized him from visits to the police station. He must have been on good enough terms with the department to get information similar to what I did. Where he got his reputation was beyond me. If looks were indicative of character, he appeared to have fallen a long way.

"I'm here, Stover. What do you want?"

"You've got to keep that gorilla off me." I stared at him blankly, in abject confusion over his non-sequitur. "Smathers. He doesn't want me to find them."

"You know, Stover, I only speak English, some Hebrew, and a bit of Yiddish. I'm not catching you. You're going to have to translate for me."

"The lady—"

"Mrs. Sylvia Morgan-Smith?"

"Yeah. She hired me to find two dames from her past. Pretty cagey about it. Gave me their names, a little bit of description probably based on what they used to look like, but nothing else. I visit her place a couple of times—" A twig snapped in the distance as though from a footfall. We waited in silence until any threat dissipated.

"Go on," I encouraged.

"So, I go up to her place a couple of times, you know, trying to squeeze out enough info to do the job. She's offering big cabbage so I want to do my best, you know? But that goon she calls a chauffeur keeps looking at me like a lion looks at an elk. I noticed him on my tail a couple of times. I don't think he's too keen on me finishing this thing up. It's almost like he wants to finish me."

"Mrs. Morgan-Smith hired me to find you, telling me you were her companion and that you simply took off."

We both looked at each other and tried to fathom the real story behind all of this. While I sensed Liam Smathers was suspect in many ways, he came across as devoted and loyal more than scheming and underhanded, in spite of his appearance and supposed background. We seemed to be at cross purposes. If Art Stover was hired to find missing persons, he would not be one himself. Unless his results led to a discovery which our mutual client found inappropriate.

As quickly as I thought that, I could hear my father in the back of my mind cautioning against judgment. Unfortunately, the current situation required as quick a calculation as possible.

"Who are these women she hired you to find?" I asked.

"Jessie Clarkson and Georgette Finster. I've got a line on Finster that she's somewhere in Joplin. I know people there. Could probably track her down in a day or two. But I did actually locate the Clarkson dame up in Newton. Boy, is she a boozer. Lives in a dump worse than mine."

"I find that hard to believe." That slipped out. There was no call for me to make a commentary on Mr. Stover. He shrugged off the comment with a smirk.

"Doesn't matter if she's on the sauce or dry, it takes

a bit with her to get a mouthful that makes sense. She kept referencing she had enough to spill the beans but on what or who I don't know. She don't say nothin' straight."

Just recently, I worked with a goniff named Max Burke, a decent fellow at heart but solely on the make for a quick buck. While I appreciated every man needed to do something to make a living and eat, I would have preferred to maintain more professional relationships. In this case, I had two options: tell Mrs. Sylvia Morgan-Smith I was unsuccessful and return the retainer, or try to make sense of this with Art Stover.

Since he was concerned about Liam Smathers, I suggested he make his way to Joplin to find Georgette Finster. After he gave me an address, I would revisit with Jessie Clarkson and determine if I could translate any of her gibberish into a reasonable and coherent statement. Stover was grateful for the assistance and indicated we would work out the financial arrangements later. I was less concerned about that and more about finding the truth in all of this.

My client, her employee, and a hired detective. Three people, each perhaps with their own motivations. I stood in the center of the triangle as I tried to maintain my balance. For now, it was more like being closer to the edge.

Chapter Five

I was grateful to have my 1942 Pontiac Torpedo Coupe, a gift from King Mar, the color of which resulted in Karla Duggan referring to it as the Sir Pounce-mobile. For this case, I would need more than the services of one of the local hack drivers.

Before I left for Newton and this encounter with Jessie Clarkson, which could possibly take a good portion of the afternoon, I knew I needed to contact Eileen. Our pleasant afternoon in the park ended with me basically instructing her to keep her nose out of this assignment. I recognized how harsh I was. While I appreciated her eagerness for my work, I knew that so many aspects of my profession could become dangerous. So much of human nature is hidden behind masks we all wear. Truth is a treasure to be dug in the hard earth. To be perfectly honest, Eileen was the paragon I tried so hard to protect.

"Why are you going up to Newton?" I got hold of her at work from a payphone in a drugstore on North Lawrence Road.

"It's part of this case."

"Well, I've got some info on this Art Stover guy—"

"I found him."

"What?" I sensed the distinct sound of disappointment in her voice, as though the air quickly escaped from a punctured tire.

"But since you are extremely diligent, there is something I need you to find for me." As long as I could keep her out of harm's way, I knew her assistance would be useful.

"What?" The response had the same tone as the prior one.

"Can you dig up from the newspaper's morgue any known associates of Eddie Adams who might still be in Wichita, or anywhere in Kansas for that matter?"

She acquiesced, but didn't sound as excited as being in a high-speed car chase down Douglas Avenue. I promised her dinner when I got back, and she made me promise it wouldn't be the Pan American. I demurred on the second part.

It took close to an hour to get to Newton, another fifteen minutes or so to track down the rooming house on the corner of South Ash Street and Southwest Second Street It was an area of town close to the railroad tracks with not too many other honest businesses around. Perhaps to some, the train whistles were like a shofar of hope.

It was barely eleven in the morning but already quite warm. The wind blew hot gusts in my face. It was as though I approached a cauldron with the intention of barring my way. I had a feeling this visit would just suck me back in.

A water-stained cardboard listing hung on the door frame, certainly nothing like a mezuzah. There were no doorbell buttons to push. I determined J Clarkson was in 2B. As I climbed the stairs, my hands found dust on the railing. My guess was the residents took root and hardly moved or left, likely due to circumstance and not desire. It reminded me of a morgue.

On the second floor, there were doors to the left and right. I knocked vigorously on the door marked 2B. Since Art Stover indicated the lady was prone to drinking, I figured she would need to be jolted to get her attention. It required a second and third attack to finally get a response.

The door opened enough for me to see half of a woman's face. The one eye had deep bags underneath and was bloodshot. The skin had a death-like pallor, not completely white but drained of blood, of vivacity, of life. This was a walking ghost. To see the other half of the face would not change my opinion.

"You Jessie Clarkson?"

She nodded.

"Can I come in?"

She shrugged and walked inside as though she didn't hear me or didn't care. Or perhaps both. By the time I got inside, she sat in a stained upholstered wing-back chair near the window that overlooked the alley. There was some kind of drink in a glass, and she just lit a cigarette.

My first thought was how easy it would be for someone nefarious to enter and kill her. Upon further inspection of the dilapidated room, I had to consider that, in some way, she was already dead. I sat on the end of the bed as there was no other chair in the room.

"Do you know Mrs. Sylvia Morgan-Smith from Wichita?" I asked bluntly.

"Nope." She drew hard on the cigarette, blew the smoke even harder in my general direction, and then took a sip of her drink.

"She knows you and she's been looking for you."

"Is that a fact?" Her tongue was thick with

drunkenness, a kind of blasé devil-may-care spirit, perhaps, as Art Stover indicated, based on possession of some arcane knowledge, a kind of intellectual talisman to safeguard her life. Either that or a complete utter lack of interest in what happened from one moment to the next. "Well, she knows where to find me. Everybody does."

If that were true, there would have been no need for Stover to be hired or me to be hired to find Stover. On top of that, if Jessie Clarkson claimed she didn't know Morgan-Smith, how could she say she knew where to find her? These were not the mystical words of Malachi or Hosea but the befuddled mutterings of one whose past hung heavy around her neck.

"How's about you tell me what this is all about?" My ears caught the voice of Jimmy Cagney, as though I were a tough guy from a Warner Brothers movie.

She leaned forward, as seductively as she was capable of, and leered at me with eyes that were now big and awake and alive.

"How's about you slip me a fin?" She raised her eyebrow in anticipation.

"How's about I slap you into sobriety?" Naturally, I would not have done such a thing but I knew I needed to take a hard line with her. She was lost in an inebriated world which gave her the kind of comfort she could not find elsewhere. Coddling her and giving in to her dissipation would have lost any thread I could pick at.

She sat back in frustration.

"You a copper?"

"Private."

"Like the other one?" She probably meant Art Stover.

"Yeah."

She let out a frustrated gasp as though she were fed up with all of us. She chugged the remnants of the glass and then poured another three fingers worth from a bottle whose label peeled off. She lit another cigarette, and left the first one to smolder in an ashtray. After a strong pull, she looked at me spitefully.

"I need money."

"For what?"

"To leave this burg."

"You'd just drink it up."

"No. I want out. I need out."

"What do you know?"

"I know who Sylvia Morgan-Smith is."

For the next ten minutes, I prodded Jessie Clarkson to give me the details of a fabulous story she had buried inside her. I didn't have the time to write it all down because it came in scattered pieces, like shards of glass broken under a huppa. I had to catch what I could and hope I would remember enough to string it all together into a statement that made sense.

She took sips throughout her recitation but that wasn't what caused her to fade into a sulking silence. It was the verbal realization of how doomed she was under the weight of a dark history. I put a five-dollar bill on the table next to her bottle, for whatever good it was going to do.

I sat in the car and scribbled a few brief notes on an envelope and tried to list a series of names that were referenced. Between Karla Duggan and my connections on the Wichita Police Department, I hoped to be able to connect ancient history with the present.

The gracious gift King Mar gave me did not come

equipped with any kind of air-conditioning system. I opened both driver's and passenger's windows on the way home and tried to keep as much of the sweat off me as possible. While I focused on my driving, it occurred to me I acquired a lot of hearsay commentary from a woman who was likely a dipsomaniac and whose testimony would be unreliable in any court. That being said, I wasn't a lawyer and no longer a cop.

It was just after one o'clock in the afternoon when I got to police headquarters on William Street. It felt even hotter now although the wind had died down a bit. Because of that I could hear every sound from all around me. Footfalls on sidewalks. A mother and her teenage daughter arguing. The traffic on main street. The city was alive with a kind of normal chaos.

Floyd Gunsaullus, Gunny to most who knew him, was a mentor and one of the best policemen I had ever known. A former motorcycle patrolman, he was now Commander of Traffic Safety. His instincts and ability to put things into perspective were the kind of resource you could find nowhere else.

"Eddie Adams? That's old news. Kind of like Herman Barker and Porter Meeks back in '27. You want to talk about dangerous criminals? How about Figueroa and Facinelli?"

"Never heard of them." I smiled in anticipation of a good story.

The look on his face was that of a cat who caught a mouse in his trap. The opportunity to spin a yarn from 'back in the day' for a youthful listener was just too much to bear.

"You heard of the St. Valentine's Day Massacre, right?"

"Yeah, of course."

"Well, that was a screw-up because the main target, Bugs Moran, wasn't there at the time. One of his associates dressed the same way and the lookout assumed it was him. Well, you got the newspapers and that dramatic photo and everyone is up in arms. Including Capone. Moran sent whatever gang members remained out of town hoping he could keep them safe and then put everything back together when the heat died down. You remember Baron Witherspoon, right?"

"Yeah. I met him briefly in '38 when he was up here on the Ripper killings."

"Well, he dealt with one of them Moran guys. A slickster named Jake Hickey. 'Crazy Jake' they called him. That bad boy got killed in Ark City back in '34, I think it was."

It was fascinating to hear Gunny recoup the events of criminal history in Kansas, but I got impatient for the meat of the story, especially given I was more interested in Eddie Adams.

"So, who were Figueroa and Facinelli?"

"Two guys Capone hired to come to Kansas looking for the remnants of Moran's gang after they took care of the yahoos who botched the job in Chicago. There were four unsolved killings in Emporia and two in Topeka in 1930. Those departments had nothing to go on. When they wound up in Wichita in '31, the FBI apparently figured out it was those guys. From the files, they were straight from Italy, good friends with Mussolini, not too bright but very brutal. No compassion, no empathy. They didn't understand the meaning of those words. All they knew was death. They were like sharks with Tommy guns. There was a shootout at the Stockyards and those two were cut to ribbons. They got what they deserved if you ask me."

"How come I've never heard of them?"

"Because the Feds came in and scooped up the bodies and told the commissioner and the chief of police they were deaf and dumb. And that, as they say, was that."

I caught my breath as I took it all in. The Peerless Princess of the Plains had its fair share of bad men who traipsed through its history. The fine citizens slept well, especially when they weren't told about all this mayhem.

After I gathered my mental composure, I got Gunny to focus on my inquiry and rattled off a list of names from my scribbling on the envelope. There were a couple he knew off the top of his head, a few that "sounded familiar," and one that was unknown to him: Sally Minter. He copied down the names and said he would have a clerk dig up records from the 1921 case and get back to me.

Eileen would get off from work in about forty-five minutes. That gave me just enough time to get to my apartment and feed the cats, as I figured to be out for the remainder of the evening if everything went as planned. Coming home late to hungry cats was a recipe for catastrophe. As it was, Sir Pounce was incessant with his mewing while Lady Mittens acted a bit more demonstrative. I gave them an extra portion for dinner and then, as humans are wont to do with pets, advised them that I would be seeing Eileen shortly. It was my misguided attempt to assure them my departure was worthwhile.

Chapter Six

I picked up Eileen outside of the Beacon Building right at five. She held some thick sheets folded in half and had an air of exuberance about her. Perhaps she considered this an internship into a world she only really knew about through movies. In any case, her enthusiasm faded as we pulled into the back lot of the Pan American Café. Her face went slack and clearly exhibited a sense of utter disappointment.

"King Mar is a good friend of mine," I said plaintively, "and the food is good. It might not be the most romantic place. Then again, we're not Nick and Nora Charles."

She harumphed out of the car and almost stomped her feet as we walked in. By second nature, I went immediately to the back booth, the one closest to the kitchen, where I always enjoyed a degree of privacy. King Mar came over to this country sometime in the 1920s but still hadn't brought his wife over. He appeared like a western Kansas wind, a huge smile plastered to his face, and kept it there in spite of Eileen's obvious dissatisfaction. He knew when to turn on the charm.

"Ah, you brought the lady tonight," he said graciously.

"I'm famished. How about one of those stacked roast beef sandwiches with a side of cole slaw?"

"Very good. And I have something special for the

lady," he declared as he turned toward Eileen and maintained the generous smile. "Matzoh ball soup."

Eileen squashed a laugh, but it still squeezed out as a stifled smirk. The notion of a Chinese man offering a Jewish delicacy was worthy of incredulity.

"It's from Harold's father's recipe," King Mar went on. "Trying to draw in more Jewish folks here. Give them a place to go on Christmas." He knew how to improve all aspects of his business.

"Your father's recipe?" she asked after King Mar left with our orders.

"Long story. So, what have you got?" I tried to get this conversation moving in the right direction.

She pulled out those papers and neatly unfolded them, undid the crease so they would lay flat. According to the old papers in the Beacon's morgue, the Wichita police rounded up as many known associates or general acquaintances after Eddie Adams was killed in a shootout on November 22, 1921. A policeman, Charles Hoffman, was killed at that time, while another, Charles Bowman was wounded. It was officer D.C. Stuckey that shot Adams three times and killed him. The ragtag gang included petty crooks and World War I veterans, none of whom had an inclination toward murder. They also ran with prostitutes and other loose women. Not what you would consider prime candidates for Sunday church services.

"One of those guys was a bootlegger named George McFarland," she eagerly reported.

"Yeah, they called him Chubb."

She was surprised by my comment.

"He was killed recently."

"I know about him. Who else?"

She was non-plussed but continued.

"A small-time crook named P.D. Orcutt was killed…"

"I found out about him, too."

Eileen practically slapped her hands on the table in complete frustration.

"What did I do all this work for if you already knew about them?"

"I don't know about everybody. Just those two. I promise. Who else was there?"

She looked and acted grumpy and obviously wondered if I would further impact her diligent efforts on top of bringing her to a restaurant she initially had no desire for.

"A guy named William, or Billy, Fintelman and his wife died in a house explosion in Fort Worth. Article said it was a gas leak. No foul play indicated. George Weisberger was one of three guys who escaped with Adams from the Kansas State Penitentiary that got this whole robbery and killing spree started. He was killed in a hit-and-run in Oklahoma City. They never caught the driver but did find the car. The real kicker was a gal named Nellie Miles. She was a pretty successful madam and long-time friend of Eddie Adams. Found dead in a car near Park Villa last fall."

"Anybody still alive or that the police didn't get to talk to?"

"Frank Foster is serving life in prison. So is D.C. Brown." She was almost finished before she went on to the last page. "Oh, yeah, there were three what you'd call good-time girls who kind of fell off the map. Georgette Finster, Jessie Clarkson, and Sally Minter."

I almost gasped. After I got my breath, I recapped

my encounter with Jessie Clarkson, explained how Art Stover attempted to locate Georgette Finster, and told her about my meeting with Gunsaullus that brought up the name of Sally Minter without any further information. She might be unknown but she popped up time and again. The buildup of tension was temporarily interrupted by a waiter bringing us food.

From my past culinary experiences, I knew the roast beef sandwich would be superb. Eileen was about to make a further observation when she stopped after the first sip of the matzoh ball soup and exclaimed it to be as good as her own mother's. High praise for a Chinese man. Looks like our people would have a decent place to go for dinner on Christmas after all.

"So, Jessie Clarkson references Sally Minter but Gunny had never heard of her?" Eileen asked for clarification.

"Doesn't surprise me all that much. There were likely lots of ladies of that type milling about and associating with thugs and gangsters. Hard to keep up with any of them. Maybe a pandering or soliciting charge here or there but nothing that would stick."

Eileen put down her spoon, then gently patted her mouth with her napkin. She crossed her hands in front of her.

"What I don't get is why you didn't just let Mrs. Morgan-Smith know you found Art Stover." I tried to answer but she continued on. "I'm noticing a pattern here, Bergman. You get hired by people who give you good money but then go against their will and seek, I don't know, something else."

"Good money? '*Wealth gotten by vanity shall be diminished; but he that gathereth by labour shall increase*.' There is all kinds of money in the world."

"In the Pirke Avot, didn't Rabbi Joshua ben Perachya admonish us to judge everyone favorably?" she retorted.

I could hear the deep breath I took before I responded, "Ezekiel 7:27 – *I will do unto them after their way, and according to their deserts will I judge them*."

I put down my sandwich and wiped my mouth when I realized it wasn't prudent to use Jewish ideology to play tennis with a woman who was very close to my heart and just as knowledgeable. To my surprise, I let out a little laugh.

"What is so funny?" she asked, extremely seriously.

"Most couples have tiffs regarding trivial matters. Look at us."

"We're not most couples." She went back to her soup without further comment on the use of the word 'couples.'

We allowed the remainder of the meal to pass in silence, as much to enjoy the repast as to allow the fog of uncertainty and determination to dissipate. It was a smart approach to take. During the quiet moments, I realized that I had perhaps been too judgmental yet again. It was one thing to dig deeply into human nature with a desire to understand it. Yet, all actions and retribution come from Adonai. We are, as we should be, merely the tools of the Divine.

When King Mar returned to the table, Eileen was overly enthusiastic in her praise. It was then I realized taking her more often would no longer be an issue. I was grateful as much to my father and his recipe as to King Mar for his willingness to prepare it.

"Harold, I'm just worried that you are going down a

path where you see yourself as an avenging angel."

"That is not my intention. I go into each case with sincerity, honesty, and integrity. Sometimes, my investigation does not always yield the same. If I find iniquity, it is not being an avenging angel to see it punished. Is it?"

She took the high road in this by not pursuing the discussion. For the moment, it appeared she would wind up as my protecting angel while I went about digging through the detritus of criminals from the past. It seemed that someone's arm reached forward into today.

I drove Eileen home. We sat in the car in silence for a bit. I tried to think of the proper thing to say. Words had come easy to me when it came to just about everyone else. Of late, I was so concerned about pushing her away inadvertently. This time, she spoke first.

"Do you know that I really think I love you, Harold Bergman?"

I turned to her, a warm smile glowing on my face.

"I was getting that impression, Miss Horowitz."

She leaned in and kissed me. *For thy love is better than wine.* Like a flash, she was out of the car and up to the steps of her apartment building. She looked back and blew a kiss, then disappeared inside.

"I really don't deserve you," I said to myself.

My foresight in providing the cats with an early dinner served me well. I came home to warm greetings, long stretches, and gentle purring. I took off my shoes and hung my jacket in the closet before I plopped on the bed still fully clothed and gave Sir Pounce and Lady Mittens the opportunity to have me to themselves for a bit.

We were aware of two prostitutes, one who provided

a name who was unknown to any of us, and the other looked for by Art Stover. If Georgette Finster could independently corroborate the name “Sally Minter,” we could assume she might be the key to what Sylvia Morgan-Smith sought.

However, as I turned it over in my head, I realized I didn’t feel all that comfortable with Stover’s original explanation. While I could tell from his demeanor he was nobody’s idea of an intellectual companion, I still had to wonder why one rich dame would hire two men for essentially the same thing. She had to know I would track down the same things as Stover in order to locate him. On top of that, his midnight meeting reeked of fear and uncertainty. Getting him out of town served two purposes. First, locating the woman in question. The second was to place the focus squarely on me.

Another thing stuck in the back of my mind. From my training on the police department, I could spot a tail. The morning trip to Newton revealed a gray two-door coupe. It could have been anybody. If I hadn’t noticed it as it passed me when I got the police station in the afternoon, I would have thought little of it.

Did they follow me or try to locate Jessie Clarkson? Or perhaps someone altogether unknown to me? I could only hope Art Stover acted as cautiously.

Chapter Seven

I awoke with a smile and thoughts of Eileen Horowitz rather than a twenty-five-year-old crime spree. It made me wonder where my focus was and where it should be. I stared straight into the mewing face of Sir Pounce which readjusted my sensibilities quite quickly.

I brewed a pot of coffee, scrambled some eggs, and made some toast. My plan was to confront my client to give her just enough of the information I gathered thus far in order to see how she responded, in keeping with my professional responsibilities. This, I hoped, would inform how I should proceed. It was while I cleaned up, I got a knock on the door. Detective Clarence Mendenhall, from the Night Detective Squad, looked less tired than usual. That might have meant he had no deep disturbing cases on his docket.

"We got a call from the Joplin Police Department," he said matter-of-factly.

"Oh?"

"They were questioning a guy name Art Stover. Local private dick, not nearly as classy as you."

"Thanks."

"Don't mention it. He was surveilling an apartment when the local patrol pulled up after getting an anonymous tip."

"A tip about what?"

"Murder."

It is a stark word. It can't be pronounced elegantly or with any flamboyance. The dictionary says it is the killing of another human being. The Bible calls it a sin. The irony was it appeared justified to soldiers in a war. My thoughts raced as I wondered about the facts. They were all that was important now.

"Who was it?"

"A dame named Georgette Finster. This Stover acted suspicious, so they naturally brought him in." There was a brief pause before he continued. "He claimed he was working a case with you."

Mendenhall was an old friend and cohort as well as an excellent cop. He didn't have to claim anything, make an accusation or even an innuendo. He just said what he said and waited for a response. Funny how I planned to do the same thing with my client. The learned acorn does not fall too far from the tree.

"Our respective interests have crossed paths." It was not the most sophisticated response, but I couldn't just pass along the stale comment about client privilege with Clarence. I respected him too much. I hoped he would offer me a similar courtesy.

He looked at me for a moment. It was the same look he gave a guy he dragged in for questioning. It was blank, mostly straightforward, but with a touch of a gleam in his eye.

"Well, you'll be happy to know they couldn't pin a thing on him and cut him loose a few hours ago. Seems this gal was dead a good twenty-four hours before Stover blew into town."

"Cause of death?"

"Strangulation. It appears she had severe bruising on her neck. Whoever did it was big and strong and mean.

Didn't like her or maybe didn't like working girls in general. Either way, the crime scene looked pretty brutal according to the detective in charge."

The last comment was a surprise to me. I never considered her or Jessie Clarkson were office secretaries but to have it stated so bluntly disturbed me quite a bit. I thanked Mendenhall for stopping by and filling me in on this. I figured Stover would drive in a panicked state and likely return to town in about four or five hours. That would give me enough time to see what my client might say.

The beautiful automobile, that designation of wealth and class, was not in the driveway. If Smathers weren't around, it might take a while for the doorbell to be answered, if at all. It was nearly five minutes before the heavy door was opened to reveal Mrs. Slyvia Morgan-Smith. She wore a heavy velvet dress and a high-collar silk blouse with a Wedgewood cameo pin. Her feet were adorned with laced-up suede boots with a heel. It would have been an immaculate wardrobe were it fall. For the second week in July, I could only wonder how she could breathe without fainting.

She guided me into the parlor where we sat as we did when I first met her. A sterling silver tea service was arranged on the low table as though she expected me. I did not hear Smathers.

"Do you have anything favorable to report, Mr. Bergman?"

"Why, yes." I looked around uncomfortably while I sipped my tea. I exaggerated my confused state so she would comment. And she did.

"Something wrong, Mr. Bergman?"

"Just wondering where Mr. Smathers is."

"He's running errands for me."

I didn't bother to ask whether those were in town or not.

"I was contacted by Mr. Stover a couple of nights ago. He wanted me to meet him at a rather obscure location. At midnight, no less. All very odd." I gave it my very best Jimmy Stewart innocent pondering. Too bad they didn't present acting awards to private detectives.

"So, he's fine then?" Her concern was less maternal and bordered on the selfish.

"He seemed to be. No signs of physical impoverishment. He simply stated he had rather urgent business to attend to and wanted me to pass along his apologies for the abruptness of his departure. Overall, very conciliatory and apologetic."

She took a deep breath as a token sign of consideration before a rather quick exhale. A slight smirk indicative of contemplation lit on her face. At last, she spoke.

"Well, your efforts have been commendable."

The acquiescence caught me completely off guard. When you are hired to find someone, it typically would require proof of any degree of success, whether it was simply photographic or producing the individual, alive or dead. This woman took me completely at my word and seemed to accept it as gospel. She was either pixilated, frivolous with her money, or a rather scheming lady. It was impossible to discern which.

"You're not originally from Wichita, are you, ma'am?" It was a pleasantly offered comment, designed to quickly change the subject, and perhaps get her to reveal some minor detail before I was forced to depart the premises. “I say this only because I have encountered no one of your grace and charm who is from here.”

Her smile was filled with the audacity of ego.

“I moved here from Kansas City, oh, fifteen years ago after the passing of my husband, Jonathan.”

“Oh, I’m so sorry to hear that. That must have been quite hard on you.”

“Indeed.”

“What did your husband do?”

“He was a banker.”

The gaiety of the conversation seemed to fall flat, like a pigeon shot out of the sky. A few passing comments I now had to look into, despite, once again, the case being closed. After all, I had located Art Stover and therefore my professional services were no longer needed. This was Albert Whitman all over again.

I thanked her for the generosity of the retainer, made the same casual comments about my availability for herself or her friends if such was required, and then offered to see myself out. I knew she would not come after me but might peek out of the windows. A quick and circumspect inspection of the garage revealed it to be empty which only verified Smathers’ absence but not to where or for how long.

A quick stop by the Carnegie Library took longer than anticipated when I found Karla Duggan in an intense conversation with a young man in his twenties who seemed intent upon monopolizing her time. At least in her mind. I was told, by her no less, I had the patience of a saint. There were no saints in Judaism, only Hasidim, and no miracles were attributed to them. I would have to remain merely pious and patient.

“Jonathan Smith or Jonathan Morgan-Smith.

Banker. Kansas City. 1931."

"Anything special about the year?" she inquired.

"Obituary."

She smiled, turned on her heel, and walked to the area where the old newspapers were kept. I guessed she would have been more expedient if it weren't for the effort to stay away from the obnoxious young feller. I busied myself with the current day's paper. Detroit had beaten the Yankees in a shutout, 2-0, with New York hurler Spud Chandler taking the loss. The United States Senate approved a nearly four-billion-dollar loan to the United Kingdom, which averted that country's bankruptcy. Members of the 442nd Regiment were awarded a Presidential Distinguished Unit Citation in a White House ceremony presided over by President Harry Truman. The unit was comprised almost entirely of second-generation American soldiers of Japanese ancestry. These Nisei were the truest definition of 'patriotism' when one considered many soldiers still had family members in internment camps. The irony was too much to consider at the moment.

Karla returned, notepad in hand, pencil behind her ear. She made eye contact with the young gentleman as a way to indicate she had someone else to attend to.

"Jonathan Smith. Born January 5, 1870. Died February 2, 1931. President of New Republic Bank and Trust from 1912 until his death. Obituary indicates rumblings about associations with T.J. Pendergast." She stopped for a moment and looked at me. "Can you believe this guy's name is Jonathan Smith? I mean, really. John Smith?"

I moved my hand in a come-hither gesture to get her to continue.

"Obit references widow, Sylvia," she went on. "Indicates they were married close to nine years."

"Did you happen to find a wedding announcement from 1922 or 1923?"

"Nope. Must have been a private ceremony."

"Yeah, but bigwigs like this get their names in the social columns even if it's a private affair. You know, the bride's gown, the size of the cake, all the famous guests."

"Wouldn't know a thing about it." That was the end of that conversation.

I calculated my former client in her early to mid-sixties, she would have been in her late forties at the time of her husband's passing and, conceivably, her late thirties when they met. My brain flashed the year 1921 in front of my eyes. Eddie Adams' ghost made an unexpected appearance.

The expenditure of thought created a powerful hunger. I circled back and went to King's X. Jennie Palmer did double duty, both waiting on tables and serving behind the counter. She graduated from high school only a year earlier, but no one could guess that who didn't already know her. She had the sensibility of a street urchin and the sassiness of a woman two to three times her age. She kept her ears open and her mouth shut. This made her an invaluable resource. She acted like a younger sister who tried to keep her older brother out of trouble.

Today, all I needed was a grilled cheese sandwich and a cup of coffee. She told me in passing the regular waitress called in sick which she actually suspected was a hangover. Jennie didn't seem to mind. Most folks would see the weariness she put on her face like a mask and tipped her exceedingly well. As she stood behind the counter, a brief nod of the head was an indication someone approached behind me.

"You're the shamus? Bergman?"

The man was even shorter than me, somewhere in his early fifties, thinning black hair with eyes that drooped like a bloodhound but didn't necessarily look sad. He hadn't shaved in a couple of days which exaggerated the wrinkles in his cheeks. Something in life wore him to a frazzle. The gray suit was clean but a good fifteen to twenty years old. It made him look even older.

"I'm Bergman."

"You choosy about your clients, Mr. Bergman?"

"As long as they can pay. I do honest work. I'm not interested in stepping over the line. Just so you know."

He looked me over like a scientist examining a petri dish.

"I didn't catch your name," I continued.

He paused for a bit. Either he tried to decide whether to identify himself or remember who he was.

"Finney. Julius." He continued to stare at me, uncertain as to whether to continue. "I done a spell up in Lansing. Got out ten years ago. Just so you know."

"I got nothing against a man who has paid his debt to society."

The sound out of his mouth was a cross between a frustrated laugh and an expulsion of hot air. It was neither friendly nor warming. It sounded more like a dying hyena with a bone to pick.

"Is that what they call it?"

I didn't want to get into a deeply ethical discussion with a prospective client regarding the morality of the judicial and penal system in this country. He had his opinions from behind the walls; I had mine while walking a beat.

"What were you in for?" I asked politely. I lowered my voice to avoid sounding confrontational.

"Armed robbery. Cullison, Kansas. February the eleventh, nineteen hundred and twenty-one."

It was the recitation of a formerly institutionalized man. There it was again: 1921. Everything circled around to that year and perhaps to Eddie Adams. Was this Julius Finney merely a coincidence?

"Why is it you need the services of a private detective, Mr. Finney?"

"I need you to find someone. You can do that, can't you?"

I nodded affirmatively. "That's what I do. Someone from back in the day you lost touch with?"

"You might say that. More like someone who ran off on me."

I detected an inherently suspicious intent about the remark. Perhaps I watched too many Dick Powell movies.

"If this individual was in possession of stolen goods or money, I'm afraid I can't help you. That would be a matter for the police."

"Nothing of the sort, friend. Just a lady who promised she'd be there for me."

It was there his voice lowered, dipped into a kind of nostalgic melancholy. He convinced me enough to proceed further.

"Who's the lady?"

"Her name is Sally Minter."

Chapter Eight

There were three good-time girls, frails, twists, muffins. Maybe professionals, likely not. But one of them Clarence Mendenhall specifically referred to as a prostitute. That was the recently deceased Georgette Finster in Joplin, Missouri. Strangled and beaten with a furious passion. Jessie Clarkson, who would not be found saying novenas in church, had a meaningful discussion with me in Newton, Kansas, pieces of which made a certain degree of sense. Now the name Sally Minter came up again. Eileen found references to her in the newspaper. Floyd Gunsaullus was not familiar with the name. My new client, Julius Finney, wanted me to find her. I would have wanted to find her even before he appeared behind me in King's X, but I was in the market for another client, one that would validate my continued investigation. This time I would be paid for being a noodge.

"I get twenty-five dollars a day plus expenses, all of which are completely itemized."

"I'm familiar with the routine, shamus" Finney replied in a very bored manner.

"What can you tell me about this Minter gal?"

"You know the American Legion Hall over on St. Francis?"

"Yeah."

"Used to be the Arlota Dancehall. We hung out there

a lot in the early twenties. She had a background but so did I. Figured I could make an honest woman out of her."

There was a kind of passing sincerity to his story but it was more based on what he wanted to believe than what likely happened. If we tell ourselves something often enough, it becomes true, at least to us. When the vision clears, reality is like a cold slap in the face. Maybe that was what all those years behind bars did to him.

"Until you got pinched and did a stretch," I responded with brutal honesty. It shook him out of his nostalgic reverie.

"You think you can find her?" he asked sharply and straight to the point.

"If I can't get a lead in two days, I won't string you along."

"You go as far along as you need to, flatfoot. I've got the cabbage and I've got the time." He pulled a folded wad from his pocket and peeled off two twenties and a ten before he turned and left. It wasn't necessary for him to give me the palaver about him finding me as opposed to the other way around. To his kind, that was standard. We understood each other completely.

I tossed a dollar onto the counter and waited until Finney crossed the street, walked east along First Street just past the Orpheum Theater. After he crossed South Topeka Street, he wound up turning down the alley that would have brought him behind the Midian Shrine Center. He didn't hear the car horn blaring behind me; I did.

Art Stover raced up and pulled over to the curb. My chances of tailing Julius Finney were gone now so the least I could do was figure how to help Stover put out whatever fire he headed for. I leaned into the passenger's window.

"That Finster dame is dead."

"I know."

"How do you know?" he asked, halfway between perplexed and upset. I recapped my conversation with Mendenhall. His anger deflated but he still rattled a bit.

"So, how did you know where to find her?" I questioned, as much out of professional curiosity as anything else.

"I told you. I had a line on her."

It was a pat comment but not the answer I expected. I let the air chill between us for a bit.

"Sally Minter." The name was stated as though I simply read it from a newspaper, maybe even an obituary. I let it hang in the silence for a moment.

"Who's that?" Now, the guy who previously played the part of a hard-boiled private dick acted like an impertinent child, the one who claimed to not know who broke momma's vase.

"Apparently a friend of the Finster and Clarkson gal. They ran together back in the day."

"Where did you get the name from?" His words came sputtering like water from a garden hose when you first turn it on. I stared at him without answering.

"I still have a hard time understanding how you located Georgette Finster and why you just sat outside her apartment. Did you go in and find her dead? Or maybe Liam Smathers tailed you and you were scared?"

"Listen, I don't have time for this." Famous last words. Stover drove off quite as quickly as he pulled up, this time without the blaring horn but with a squeal of tires.

I walked slowly toward King's X to try to sort the

pile of information that got dumped in my lap. Sylvia Morgan-Smith hired me to find Art Stover who she hired to find Georgette Finster and Jessie Clarkson. No one mentioned looking for Sally Minter until Julius Finney approached me out of a clear blue sky. The question was why Finney would hire me and how he knew where I was. Then I recalled the gray two-door coupe that I thought tailed me up and back to Newton.

I used the phone in King's X to contact the Newton police department. I hated to throw Clarence Mendenhall's name around but I needed an expedient answer and didn't have the time to go through channels or spend half a day driving up and back. The simple question was: Had there been a recent homicide in the name of Jessie Clarkson? Thankfully, the answer was no. Yet I couldn't help to think her life was in danger. It was as though pieces of the past were systematically wiped clean in order to sew it shut. The question was: Who would do that? I figured it to be Miss Minter yet I still didn't have a handle on who she was.

I was not aware of any direct connection between the Jazz Age criminal activities and the music scene, but it could not be denied the malcontents did enjoy their dancing and libations. My dear friend, Gage Brewer, gave the first ever performance of his electric guitar, nicknamed the "Frying Pan," on Halloween night of 1932 at the Shadowland Pavilion. These days, he could be found rehearsing at the York Rite Temple, just a block from my apartment. Even if I wasn't successful finding him, I figured to head home anyway to make the usual diagrams I used to put the pieces together.

Gage was a dozen years older than me and the absolute epitome of class and charm. He had a broad smile and searing eyes, the kind that could look deeply inside you. His hair was slicked back to reveal a high forehead. Even during a rehearsal, he dressed as though it was a show in front of a full house. He could be somewhat of a taskmaster given his perfectionist nature. It all came out in the transcendent music which, for me, even a cantor in temple could not approach.

The group finished "A Good Man is Hard to Find," flowing like an easy ripple on the Arkansas River in the early days of spring. Our eyes met. I saw Gage suppress a smile. His rehearsals were akin to boot camp in their seriousness. He would offer the guys a ten after the song and greet me, but not shake my hands which were as sacred to a guitarist as the Torah was to a rabbi.

"You've missed your chance to bring your lady friend to see me," he pronounced almost with a sense of profound disappointment.

"How's that?"

"Three weeks in Oklahoma City, followed by two in Tulsa."

"So, my chance will return in five weeks?" The joviality we shared was an unbreakable bond. How easy it could be for those from different worlds to form friendships, if only they tried. "You remember the Arlota Dancehall?"

"Oh, yes. Homer Osborne played there about two years before I arrived in Wichita. Then it became the Crystal Dance Hall, then the Royal Dance Hall, and then—"

"The American Legion Hall," I interjected.

"Exactly." His face grew contemplative, likely wondering why I rehashed the history of musical venues. "You on a case?" His instincts were at their peak, as usual.

"Yeah, but it doesn't involve music. You remember a guy named Eddie Adams?"

"Before my time, but, yeah, the name gels."

There was really no reason for me to be there, no possible way this talented musician could help with any knowledge of what I looked for. Yet, sometimes, you reach out to a friend for feedback because you trust them to give you unfettered advise that is possibly better than a completely scientific analysis. A word or a thought triggers a realization or a speculation. That's what I looked for.

"If you were running with a bad crowd and you wanted out, how would you do it?" The question would make absolutely no sense to a musician. A friend, on the other hand, would give a concerted response.

"First thing I would do is move out of town."

"Good. Makes sense. Then what?"

He rubbed his chin, then looked skyward, before facing me again.

"Am I a guy or a gal?"

"You're a gal."

"Well, that makes it easier."

"Oh, yeah? How so?" This got interesting, not because of the responses but from the person who provided them. It is likely Gage Brewer never contemplated a sinister notion or criminal intention unless he was around me. To have a notion in this regard brought to light an aspect of him I had not known or considered before

"What can a guy do? If he's got a beard, he can shave it off. Takes a longer time to grow one. A fake moustache doesn't work too well up close. Maybe he can cut his hair or go bald. Change his clothes. But women change their appearances all the time. Sometimes every day. Makeup, hair styles, clothing. A woman can look like a farmer's daughter at noon and a debutante at midnight. On top of that, she can get married."

"Come on. What does that have to do with the price of tea in China?"

He pulled me closer in a kind of conspiratorial manner.

"A man can change his name but his instincts and attitude remain. When a woman marries, not only does her name change but her demeanor does as well. There are a lot of my current and former bandmates that will attest to this."

It seemed revelatory in nature. I would have to run it by Eileen for validation as she was far more familiar with the female psyche than Gage supposed he was. I simply nodded my head, patted him on the shoulder, and walked out. It was time to head home.

While a gray two-door coupe might be able to blend in with city traffic, a Rolls Royce Phantom II Continental does not. It was parked on the northeast side of the intersection of North Market Street and East Eighth Street. The driver waited for me; there could be no other reason.

Rather than get into my car and pretend not to notice, I considered it time to confront the hulking chauffeur and personal assistant of my recent client. I didn't fear him as much as Art Stover did. Outside of an exerted plea to not take on the case, he made no direct threats. So far.

"I assume you are looking for me," I said directly.

"You found Stover?"

I nodded.

"Where is he now?"

I shrugged. "Your employer was satisfied with my efforts and released me from any further obligation."

"And yet you went all the way to Newton to harass a sick woman."

"Now, you don't drive a gray two-door coupe. So how would you know that?"

"Miss Clarkson is a personal friend of Mrs. Morgan-Smith. Miss Clarkson contacted Mrs. Morgan-Smith after she indicated she was accosted by a man who was trying to get her to make false accusations against Mrs. Morgan-Smith."

It sounded very much like two opposing attorneys on a case trial. I gave Smathers too much credit for that kind of intelligence.

"Did you ever think that might have been Stover?"

Smathers realized he had overplayed his hand. His attempts to scare me off a case that he perhaps didn't realize was already closed only confirmed for me that this situation wasn't right and even more that Art Stover was in danger.

Liam Smathers made a sound like that of a petulant adolescent, then drove off, not nearly as demonstrably as Art Stover less than thirty minutes prior. At that moment, the car had more class than the driver. Nevertheless, people were unsatisfied with my responses and just drove away. I was left to assume their motives weren't on the up-and-up.

Chapter Nine

For the second night in a row, I picked up Eileen outside the Beacon building. This time I was not expected. She had a look of pleasant surprise. It would be presumptuous to assume anything greater than that.

"I really need your feedback on something," I said, leaning toward the passenger window.

"I could look up whatever you need tomorrow."

"No, this is more like, well, your perspective as a woman."

It seemed like an awkward comment to make. Her agreeable smile widened and reassured me.

"Do I get dinner with this?"

"Sure. Where?"

At this moment, for as long as I had known Eileen Horowitz, I did not know what was on her mind. Her response surprised me.

"What do you have at home?"

Granted, I recently had her over to dinner when I wrapped up the Debra Rose Nathan case. On that occasion, I spent the better part of the day in preparation to make a meal both edible and appealing at the same time. I wasn't an off-the-cuff type when it came to the kitchen nor was I all that prepared with a variety of available food. That was one attribute I did not inherit from my father.

"Well, I've got some eggs and bread."

"Ooh! How about a fried egg sandwich?"

It wasn't a taxing request. I knew I could figure it out. So I acquiesced.

We spoke little on the ride to my apartment. It would have done no good to start a heavy-handed conversation in the car. When we got there, I realized I neglected to restrain the cats behind the French doors. It was almost as though they dismissed my presence and went straight to Eileen, rubbed against her legs and accepted ear and head rubs from her. There were repeated references to Lady Mittens being a good girl and Sir Pounce being a good boy, all done in a tone typically reserved for infants. The cats ate that up almost as voraciously as their canned food, which they then turned to me for in a manner less gracious as the one they gave my guest.

I knew how to make toast and butter it. I knew how to fry eggs. This was my first fried egg sandwich. I started to dig in when a throat clearing from the other side of the table reminded me of an obligation.

Baruch ata Adonai, Eloheinu Melech ha-olam, hamotzi lechem min ha'aretz. I figured the prayer over the bread would suffice.

After we ate, I removed the plates. Eileen folded her hands under her chin and simply stared at me and patiently waited for the inquiry. She was as cute as Deanna Durbin.

"Let's say you're a gal running with a bad crowd and you want out. What do you do?"

"Well, leave town. Isn't that obvious?"

"Sure. But how? I want this from a woman's perspective. Do you hitchhike, take the train, steal a car?"

"Bus." She proclaimed it as though it were

definitive.

"Okay. Why?"

"Nobody looks at you on a bus. It's cramped, it doesn't hold a lot of people, most people who take it can't afford much more, and the driver is the only one who gets a good look at you."

I nodded. First question of the night and she made more sense than I could have expected.

"So, you live in Wichita. Where do you go?"

"Kansas City."

"Why?"

"Easy to hide there."

"Any more so than Oklahoma City or Dallas?"

She looked at me, but I could tell she didn't see me.

"Those are too 'South' in attitude. Kansas City is closer to Wichita in temperament."

"Fine. But hiding takes time and money. Both tend to run out sooner than expected."

"Ah, but the lady is going to look for a gentleman to be her guardian."

This was similar to what Gage mentioned. I liked the direction of this analysis. It didn't occur to me that my dear childhood friend had a devious plotting mind. What had I overlooked all those years?

"Will she look for the sweet innocent dentist who doesn't know about her background or someone from the darker circles of society?"

"It would be too hard for her to make up a life history and have to remember it when they get together for pinochle or contract bridge. She's looking for an easier life, not a harder one. Obviously, though, she doesn't want to be completely beholden to him. That would be just as bad as where she escaped from. How am I doing?"

I reached across the table and held her hand. "Just great." I smiled.

"When she left Wichita, did she have any money or just the clothes on her back?"

"For argument's sake, let's say she had a major stash."

"So, she's looking for someone for whom money is important while he can offer her respectability in return."

"Such as?"

"Oh, I don't know. Accountant, stock broker, banker."

She stopped right there when my face went blank.

I likely was white as the snow on Christmas day and as cold to boot. Just as she did with me, I looked straight ahead but didn't see her because my brain at that moment was like the lock on a safe as all the tumblers clicked into place.

Eileen reached for my hand. It was the warmest thing I had felt in a long time.

"I think Sylvia Morgan-Smith is Sally Minter." My voice was straight and direct. It was a declaration, not of a fact but of a realization. I then recapped everything I had been through between my trip to Newton, the information about the dead woman in Joplin, the encounters with both Art Stover and Liam Smathers, and how it all seemed to add up. I hadn't intended to include Eileen so deeply in this investigation, but she proved to be completely beneficial.

"But why did she hire you to find a man she claimed was her companion?"

"Art Stover wasn't a companion. He must have figured this lady was somehow involved with Chubb

McFarland and then learned about the other killings of people associated with Eddie Adams. My guess is he approached her with a mind for blackmail. She used me as a way to locate him so that her majordomo, that Smathers character, could eliminate him. And anyone else of consequence for that matter. Once I learned more than they considered, she cut me loose."

"That means you're in danger."

"Consider my profession, Eileen. When am I not in danger?"

It wasn't my aim to be dismissive. Given her successful theories and speculations, I needed her to remain focused so I could reach a viable conclusion.

I quickly went into my bedroom where I had a folder of information that I put together, brought it to the dining room table, and started to flip through pages of notes. I pulled one page out, then another.

"What is all that?" she asked.

"Between August and September of 1921, Adams and his gang robbed banks in Rose Hill and Haysville and got away with ten thousand dollars. They got five hundred dollars in silver from a bank near Osceola, Iowa. Their biggest heist was thirty-five thousand dollars from a Santa Fe express train near Ottawa, Kansas. Less than five hundred dollars was recovered after Adams' death and the arrest of only a couple of his known gang. Most of the rest of them eluded the police."

I closed the file folder and then suddenly beamed like a professor at Wichita University before a new dissertation.

"Sylvia Morgan-Smith married an older banker named Jonathan Smith sometime around 1922. She was widowed nine years later. Svetlana Halonen references encountering her at the Innes Tea Room in 1932. There is nothing about this woman prior to her marriage to this banker. And, as of now, there is no information available on Sally Minter."

I stared at Eileen. Perhaps I expected a response. It was just as likely I allowed my brain to cool off from the heat of rapid-fire thinking. While I couldn't allow myself to get too caught in the notion of being in danger, it occurred to me others might be impacted. Jessie Clarkson could be a loose end but after she spoke with me, it might be too obvious to do anything more than keep a steady supply of liquor in her reach. Art Stover knew the risks he took if he contemplated blackmail. Now, however, Eileen, by virtue of my sharing this information, could be a target as well. My exuberance for her involvement placed her in jeopardy as well.

"What are you going to do?" she asked.

It was a fair question. To change one's name to escape the tribulations of past indiscretions was not a crime, unless those tribulations were criminal in nature. The deaths of other associates, at least at this point, could not be directly connected to Sylvia Morgan-Smith or Liam Smathers. To reach out across several jurisdictions simply to connect the dots would be time-consuming and perhaps pointless if no interstate agency would prosecute. Might this fall under federal authority? I was too far removed from law enforcement to have an answer at my fingertips.

This mental beating I gave myself turned me into a morose host. I was hired, paid, and as many times before, delved deeper and beyond the original mandate. My sense of justice was stirred up. Yet, I found a despair due to my futility. *What profit hath a man of all his labour which he taketh under the sun?* If the purpose of my current profession was to seek the truth, perhaps I reached too far to seek justice.

"What I'm going to do is take you home and then do the dishes."

She didn't appear disappointed or overly concerned. The glow from her face, the softness of her eyes, held a profound sense of caring and, dare I say it, love. It comforted me to know I had Eileen in my life to go along with my feline companions. These truly were blessings.

I walked her to the front door to her apartment building. She noticed as I looked behind her and toward the street.

"I promise you I will be very careful," she said, as though she stared into a crystal ball or perhaps the look of worry on my face.

"I don't tell you enough how grateful I am for you. In so many ways and for so many things."

She put a finger to my lips.

"You tell me enough," she said just before she gave me a soft kiss.

I had a pleasant drive home until I opened the apartment door. The cats acted disgruntled. Perhaps Eileen's presence made them realize there were other humans who could appreciate their regal status and omnipotence even more than me. It didn't help that I spent the next twenty minutes washing dishes. I sat on the sofa to distance myself from the files that still sat on the table and beckoned me like a siren.

The smartest thing to do would be to drop all further involvement with Sylvia Morgan-Smith. An outlaw killed in Wichita twenty-five years earlier gave rise to a woman who ran away, ostensibly to save herself from any prison sentence, married a man who, despite an age difference, likely provided her with an entrée into respectable society. All else, such as the deaths of known associates, was speculative. I would not travel to Dallas or Oklahoma City or even Kansas City to talk with police departments about cases that, for them, were of lesser importance. The stories from the past remained as closed books.

The next thing to do would be to go to bed and start the next day fresh, and wait for further cases, newer jobs. Unfortunately, the loud pounding on my door prevented any of those best laid plans.

I opened the door, and Art Stover fell into my apartment with a heavy thud. He looked like he had been run over by a Sherman tank. Or perhaps a Rolls Royce Phantom II Continental. Bruising around the eyes and nose created purple and red splotches on his face. His mouth and nose bled while tears welled in his eyes. His clothes were ruffled and soiled. I couldn't tell what kind of internal injuries he might have.

I jumped over to one of my neighbors, Mrs. Cora Peacock, in apartment 101, and knocked on her door louder than I would normally have done. I knew she had a telephone. I beseeched her to contact the police, request an ambulance, and advise them it was me who made the request in hopes it would expedite the process.

It took nearly fifteen minutes before a squad car appeared with Clarence Mendenhall. The ambulance was just behind him. Several neighbors stepped out from their doors. I went around reassuring them everything was okay and that no one in the building was in any kind of danger.

St. Francis was close by. When the ambulance left

with Stover, Mendenhall stayed behind. We stepped into the apartment which was a clear signal to the neighbors the excitement had subsided, and they could try their best to get back to bed.

I gave Mendenhall the short version of events, for the moment leaving out my discoveries and speculations about my former client. My theories would not have held up in a court of law nor would they even be practical enough to secure a warrant. I just counted on his understanding and possible guidance.

Clarence Mendenhall was a good cop and a perceptive detective. He could have been my supervisor if I had decided to return to the police department after the war and joined him on the Night Detective Squad. Going by the book, whether the statutes of the state of Kansas or the Old Testament, would not provide me the answers I sought. Yet I was strangely compelled by each of them.

"Look, I know you know what you're doing," he started. "But this Stover looks like he has been beaten with a lot of anger. Whoever did this to him is not afraid of consequences. Of any kind. When rage like that is tied in with apathy, you've got a dangerous perpetrator. It would be like standing in front of an Atchison, Topeka, and Santa Fe train blaring into Union Station."

That clarified everything for me. Whatever doubts there were, whatever bits of speculation raced around inside my head finally settled into place. The problem now was to determine a resolution. The crop that was planted so many years ago was about to be harvested.

Chapter Ten

While I had complete and utter faith in Karla Duggan's research abilities, I knew I could discover something deeper and more personal by directly interviewing some people I knew right in Kansas City. While the good old Sir Pounce-mobile served me splendidly in town, we never traveled a great distance together. On the police force, I was never the partner in the squad car who drove. The sergeant of my platoon was hesitant about my use of a Jeep. This adventure in itself would be a mystery as I would soon determine whether my car was a tank or a bicycle. And whether I was a charioteer or a cartoon character.

Additionally, since I moved in and adopted my feline charges, I had not spent an inordinate amount of time away from them. While cats are more than self-sufficient, they are also emotionally more fragile than a hunting dog. I filled their bowls with extra kibble and water and could only hope for the best. I figured it would be a day at the most.

Some quick calculations after Mendenhall left indicated about a four-hour trip each way. I figured I could get there on one tank of gas and then, of course, another to get home. Hopefully, I could get all the answers I needed in one day without spending the night. All these expenses were on me. Granted, I had a substantial retainer from my now-former client to use as well as substantial funds from prior cases. This was different though. This was the use of my fee to potentially bring about the arrest of a client. I wasn't sure if that was irony or justice.

As a soldier, I had spent countless hours in what might be considered boredom. We marched, traipsed through forests and fields, followed by a bivouac for either a few hours or a few days. You knew bullets and shells could kill you. What you learned were the thoughts that roamed around in a quiet mind could be just as bad.

I realized I had to use this long period of time driving to reevaluate my beliefs, both what I thought happened and whether my response was appropriate. It was different with Albert Whitman. The task was to locate his daughter, even though the reasons seemed dubious. If I had not met with her and her beau, Dale Walker, I might have let it go once she returned to her father. I could have considered the girl indeed made an impetuous mistake. Their attitudes, however, seemed to be of a couple truly in love. In that case, I felt justified.

The search for Debra Rose Nathan had drawn me deep into a well of malicious intent that, as it turned out, had nothing to do with her disappearance. The aspect of national security touched a chord within me that brought back the reasons I gave up a career in law enforcement to fight for this country. It is a shame that tragedy often provoked patriotism.

None of that seemed to be in play here. An older lady, what one might call a dowager, hired me simply to locate a man described as a companion. That he turned out to be more than that, or rather someone other than that, was of no consequence. The fact this all related to events from twenty-five years earlier, a case brought to resolution by my former employer, the Wichita Police Department, should not have mattered. Other people died in various cities who had a tenuous connection, and most of these deaths did not appear to be connected. That alone should have dampened my resolve.

But a homicide in Joplin, Missouri, and a vicious assault on the man I was hired to locate meant the past crept into the present, with its claws and fangs firmly entrenched and unwilling to let go. While it did not impact me directly as of yet, it rankled my sense of justice and fairness. I did not care one way or another for Art Stover. The fact remained no one deserved the type of assault he received. As he fell into my apartment, I could not deny my first thoughts were of Liam Smathers. Perhaps it was too obvious and someone directed that assumption.

I left early in the morning for two reasons. The first was to maximize my daylight hours in Kansas City. The other was to avoid too much driving in what the early edition of the *Beacon* indicated would be a hot day. Along the way, I saw farmers as they harvested wheat. These were the type of folks for whom the early morning was a blessing. A kind of beauty lived in the knowledge that the toast I had for breakfast was likely made from Kansas wheat. The folks in the big cities on the East Coast likely thought bread came from a grocer.

I held, for the moment, a stillness within me, as I watched those do the tasks of their fathers, begrudging not the labor before them. While I was content with my current profession, I still did not have comfort in a way forward. The ringing echoes of Psalms 16:11 spun around in my head. *Thou wilt shew me the path of life; in thy presence is fulness of joy; at thy right hand there are pleasures for evermore.*

I had done, at least I thought, everything possible since I returned from the war to find that path. Perhaps in eschewing the sacred (in the form of the temple) and the profane (as exemplified by those encountered working for the police), I inadvertently stepped off the true path. Perhaps the Most High merely provided me with several options toward the fullness of joy.

Then suddenly, the face of Eileen Horowitz was impressed upon my mind, stuck firmly in my eyes. My childhood friend and high school crush was now an integral part of my life. She relished the notion of helping me along in this case, even knowing full well the inherent dangers. It wasn't simply the thrill of an adventure. She was intent upon the role of a partner perhaps only to safeguard me. What a remarkable thought that was. I considered she was more like a sister in our youth. As we grew and turned into the people we became, it was evident more existed within us than how things started. I was quite sure it was more evident to her earlier than it was to me.

This was where the conflict came in for me. If Eileen was the true path to fulfillment and joy, I could not continue this journey as a private investigator. While it satisfied my desire to understand and help people, it could result in serious harm that would impact a loving home permanently. I had to consider that a job would not be more important than the warmth of a household. Some might not consider my father's profession of jeweler and watch repair to be of much consequence. What was significant was he found a sense of fulfillment in his tasks and those who knew him admired his integrity. The job, such as it was, had no great import into his character.

How he approached it meant everything.

If I sold myself on this proposition completely, I would have turned the car around and returned home, perhaps reach out to Troy Harding for a position as an insurance investigator. It likely would have been a nine-to-five job with good pay as well as the opportunity to be home every night. The fact was I already proceeded more than halfway on my journey once I passed Emporia. As more of Kansas City, Kansas could be seen before me, the tranquility of the pastoral portions of Kansas faded. The urban jungle awaited. My inquiry remained.

To be as efficient as possible, I made a list of those I needed to interview. Naturally, I would start with the police. Years ago, Floyd Gunsaullus raved about a detective a few years older than himself who had a sharp mind and a memory for crime. Marcus Maxton was just on this side of sixty and fended off suggestions that he should retire. His case load was met, and he never took a day off for any health reasons. His craggy features and droopy eyes might convince you he was older than Methusaleh but there definitely still was a pep in his step. After a brief introduction and reminiscence about Gunny, he offered his assistance, perspective, and memory.

"Yeah, that Smith character was definitely tied up with the Pendergast machine. Oh, not so as you could prove anything. Lord knows, I tried."

"His money kept him safe?" I inquired.

"Money? Oh, heck no. Played the horses, threw lavish parties, lived well beyond his means. That is, until she came along."

Maxton described an alluring woman, definitely not a frail wretch and certainly far more mature, who, according to the prevailing scuttlebutt, infused the wayward banker with the capital he needed to get solvent. She, in turn, became part of the high society scene and helped clean up Mr. Smith's demeanor and reputation. It was the epitome of *quid pro quo.*

"Where did she and her money come from?" The question was the crux of my investigation.

"No one knew. On top of that, no one was saying bupkis."

"If you had to guess?"

He shook his head.

"What if she ran off with the Eddie Adams loot?"

His eyebrows got really close together like his brain was a turbine steam engine that worked on all cylinders. While the widow of Jonathan Smith no longer lived in his city and was not even remotely associated with any known crimes, Detective Maxton had an abiding interest in the possibilities. He gave the vague impression of my cats at feeding time.

We discussed the scenarios, considered various possibilities, and put together a few theories. All this was done with the knowledge we had no solid evidence. As this was yet to be considered a criminal case in Wichita, it was for the sole purpose of laying the groundwork for me to turn over some kind of an assessment to the police department. Maxton had me follow him to the basement where they kept old files.

He found a few scraps that were peripherally associated with Smith, nothing with any mention of his wife. He indicated I could likely get a copy of the marriage license from the Hall of Records, but I assumed the information about her past would be fabrication. Thomas Pendergast, the political boss, died in January of

1945. A tough old kingmaker like him would not have divulged anything had he still been alive. Perhaps a hearty guffaw or a breathy curse. All I got from this meeting was the kind of validation I was on the right path. Where it would lead would be anyone's guess.

My next stop was at the *Kansas City Star*. Eileen had gotten a recommendation for me to visit with Garrett Offerman, the long-time crime reporter. He started there after the first war and used his experiences to bring a fresh perspective. He worked his way up to the main guy who wrote about crime. Apparently, he received as many threats as offers of bribes. He wore thick glasses, held on to what hair he could, and carried around a belly that looked like a sack of laundry. He sighed and wheezed a lot but he was entirely outgoing. A talkative type, voluminous stories of the old days would fill anyone's ear he could bend.

"Well, there was nothing specific you could tie Smith to. He certainly mingled in a lot of different crowds. You know, corrupt politicos, underworld sharps, and a whole lot of bookies and gamblers. But that wife of his kept him buttoned-up." I sensed he enjoyed the reminiscing.

"Tell me about her."

"Classy dame. Not showy or flashy. Just kept to herself mostly while he shot off his mouth. However, all it took was a certain look and he'd snap it shut."

"You know where she came from?"

He looked to the ceiling in expectation of an answer to drop on his head.

"Closest thing I could figure about her past was a rumored connection to a guy named D.C. Brown."

"Wasn't he captured with Eddie Adams in 1921?"

"Exactly. And then was recaptured while Adams formed a new gang. You'd have to reach out to the boys in Lansing for those records."

"What was this rumored connection with this guy?"

Offerman described this Brown character as on the up-and-up in terms of criminal activity but he still pulled enough weight to be the go-to guy for one's needs. Somehow, he introduced Sylvia Morgan (who just might have been Sally Minter) to Jonathan Smith, acting as a kind of gangland cupid. Brown was known to have been at various social functions until he disappeared right after the start of the Great Depression.

The steps started to congeal. Sally Minter was part of Eddie Adams' circle. Perhaps she was even entrusted with the take from their various robberies. Adams was killed and various others were arrested. Sally made her way to Kansas City, located Brown who introduced her to a man of importance who had financial difficulties. The money she absconded with got him solvent while he offered her a more desirable way to disappear when she changed her name, got married, and ended up a grand society dame. Her husband died of his indulgences, and she moved to Wichita.

That part confused me. If she were comfortable and safe in Kansas City, there would be no need to move back. While it may have been a full ten years and any heat would be off, feelings of nostalgia alone would undermine the credibility she built. There had to be other reasons for her departure from the safe confines of the Pendergast machine. This was the next step on this journey.

Chapter Eleven

New Republic Bank and Trust was a cross between a Gothic castle and Fort Knox. It presented a grandeur that represented security and reliability, a place free from the ravages of the Great Depression. It was just as likely a place that safeguarded secrets as well as assets. Opening those kinds of doors would take a significantly greater effort. Often demons lurked behind stone walls.

Roland Castro seemed terribly young to be a Senior Executive Manager. Perhaps his title was loftier than his position. He dressed well and spoke well but his lack of knowledge revealed his youthful lack of experience. I assumed he would be the transition to the next generation. On first glance, he wasn't that impressive.

"Regrettably, Mr. Bergman, I was not employed at the bank during Mr. Smith's tenure as president. Nevertheless, had I any direct knowledge of his duties, we would be unlikely to discuss them without a proper reason. Backed, of course, by legal requirements."

"Of course." The words rolled off young Mr. Castro's tongue like oil, slippery and without substance. "Perhaps a more senior executive might have some recollection?"

"Perhaps. But again…" He did not complete the sentence. These types figured the repetition of his and the bank's stance was beneath his position. The only thing currently beneath him were shoes in need of a polish.

A gentleman in a double-breasted gray suit with onyx and gold cuff links and spats on his shoes approached slowly, almost silently. He was a remnant of a time when a man's wardrobe was the definitive signature of his character. This man's hair was gray, slightly lighter in color than his suit. His perfectly trimmed moustache curled up slightly in a handlebar fashion, not to the extreme of a barber from the last century. I could sense a definitive air of authority blended with grace and charm.

"Mr. Castro, I believe one of the cashiers requires your assistance." The sonorous baritone voice was low but carried weight. The words were minimal but with meaning behind them. I could see nothing at the front counter remotely indicative of a need for assistance. The younger executive understood the older gentleman's intention and walked off without so much as a farewell.

"It's Bergman, correct?"

"Yes. It is."

"An investigator of some sort?"

"Correct again."

I got the feeling he had overheard the entire conversation and was aware of my inquiry. I expected the brush-off from a more polished member of the executive staff with more formal language. I was surprised.

"Won't you follow me to my office?"

I did not have a tape measure with me but I surmised the gentleman's office was slightly more than half of my entire apartment. A red-leather winged-back chair sat calmly behind a large mahogany desk replete with a green-glass globed lamp, bronze paper holder and desk set, and photos of a comely woman, presumably his wife. There were enough leather-bound volumes on the shelves behind him to give one the impression of a lawyer's domain. The murmur of the bank lobby was entirely muffled once the door closed. This was a place of solace, a place where secrets came to die. Or be reborn.

"I'm Benjamin Thorpe, president of the bank." I wasn't convinced it was a pleasure to meet him so I did not say as much. "I understand you're looking for information about our former president, Jonathan Smith."

"That's correct."

"For what purpose?"

"Much as your institution maintains standards of privacy and discretion, my profession requires the same." I had enough of a vocabulary to volley comments back and forth. At times, it could be pleasurable. Unless time was of the essence. In this case, I had an egg timer in my head which give me just as much time as I needed but not anymore.

"Point taken. Well, since I was acquainted with Mr. Smith on a personal level, perhaps we can confer without violating either of our ethical standards."

"I would be grateful, sir."

There was a brief pause before what I assumed would be a recitation similar to a campfire story. I wasn't too far off the mark.

"I started here as a teller and then moved to a position similar to Mr. Castro's. I must admit to being even rougher around the edges. Mr. Smith saw great potential in me, and shall we say, groomed me into a responsible executive."

"Did you socialize with he and his wife?"

Another pause. He was careful to choose his words so as not to besmirch the memory of a mentor.

"I was often invited to their many functions at home. Hardly anything more than that."

He treated me like a dirty towel that a laundress tried to rinse clean. Give those linens enough soap and the stain disappears.

"What do you know about Mrs. Smith?"

"Lovely lady," he proclaimed with a fond reminiscence. "Did her best to keep Mr. Smith in line, as it were."

"He needed that?"

"Oh, yes. Here at the bank, Jonathan Smith was the epitome of financial professionalism. Highly knowledgeable and an astute deal-maker. A rare intelligence and business acumen. Outside these walls, however, was a different matter." I opened my mouth to speak but he continued quickly, "*De mortuis nil nisi bonum.*"

"Of the dead, speak nothing but good," I translated.

"Precisely. I learned a lot from Jonathan Smith to the extent that I was made president of the bank after his passing. I also learned to temper my predilections and not allow them to get the better of me. I have no intention of standing on his bones and besmirching his character."

"*The evil that men do lives after them;/The good is oft interred with their bones.* And here we are putting things in reverse order." Mr. Thorpe began to retort before I continued, "What became of Mrs. Smith after his passing?"

"She had no stomach for the big city and decided to leave."

"Where did she go?"

"Dallas."

His response was too quick given his more thoughtful prior replies. I learned that people gave a quick answer that was so far removed from the truth to misdirect your attention. Mr. Thorpe was as well versed in magic as he was finance. Perhaps they were one and the same.

The sands of the egg timer ran out. I stood, shook his hand firmly, and thanked him. I didn't wait for him to escort me out but left briskly on my own terms. My own knowledge of magic included an astute disappearing act. This charade would have dragged out into a volley of verbal acuity and a waste of my time.

At this point, all I had was supposition and speculation. Nothing concrete, no facts to tie in my assumptions to the truth. The only people who might have been in danger was Jessie Clarkson, who was oblivious to reality, and Art Stover, who stuck his neck out and should have expected to have his head cut off. Just the same, I had to admit all of this extracurricular activity might put me and perhaps Eileen in harm's way. If Sylvia Morgan-Smith was indeed Sally Minter and she meticulously removed anyone who could topple the world she created, I would no longer be looked upon as a mere nuisance but an actual threat.

The man who followed me around the city was just outside the main door to the bank. His dark suit was clean but distinctly out of fashion. While he needed a shave, he did not come across as a drunk or a vagabond. On the contrary, to be diligent enough to go from a police precinct to a newspaper to a bank made him a determined individual. Appearances can be deceiving; actions tell a greater truth.

"I'm about to head back to Wichita so if there's something you'd like to discuss, Mr. Brown, I'm all ears."

His large grin revealed a definitive need to see a dentist.

"You're a smart one, you are. Well, smart guy, you're looking for Sally Minter, aren't you?"

"You're smart as well, Mr. Brown."

"How much are you willing to pay to find her?"

It was only a matter of time before he tried to put the bite on me. It came sooner than later. I was prepared.

"Nothing. I know where she is."

"Says who?"

"Says me."

His confident smile faded. His face went through a series of contortions that matched his emotions. First anger, followed by disappointment, and then finally confusion.

"You don't know what you're talking about."

"Sally Minter leaves Wichita, then arrives in Kansas City. Sally Minter vanishes from sight and Sylvia Morgan appears and marries a banker. Sylvia Morgan-Smith, now a prominent and affluent widow, leaves Kansas City. You don't think I can guess where she went? The question is: why?"

He started to ramble in nervous excitement and defiance.

"T.J. didn't want her around anymore, didn't trust her. She had too much on the machine, all of her husband's files. Could have stopped the whole thing dead in its tracks. But Mr. P. was a gentleman, though. He straight up bought the files and told her to skedaddle.

Which she did."

As soon as the last words left his mouth, his hand flew up to cover it. In his exuberance, he gave me the last piece of the puzzle and verified for me that Sally Minter, the friend and associate of Eddie Adams, was now Sylvia Morgan-Smith, the wealthy grande dame and widow of corrupt banker Jonathan Smith.

I turned and walked away quickly. While I had no further reason to remain here, I decided I could do nothing back in Wichita. For what it was worth, the only recourse I had was to buy myself peace of mind and confront my former client. This assumed, of course, I could get past Liam Smathers.

I returned late that evening and got some paper to make a full and complete report. In it, I detailed what I discovered after being employed by Sylvia Morgan-Smith and what connections I made to a twenty-five-year-old case. I tried to include verbatim conversations to the best of my recollections. While the report was light on actual facts, I made certain to show the connections in as logical a fashion as possible. My old police training came in handy.

I folded the report and put it in an envelope. I sealed it shut and then put the envelope in a larger one and sealed it as well. It was just getting close to the bed time of my landlady, Contance Hanover so I knocked gently on her door.

"Sorry to disturb you but I do need a slight favor."

"Certainly."

"I need you to hold onto this for me."

"Why, of course. For how long?"

"Until I retrieve it. Now, if something were to happen to me—"

She gasped audibly.

I hoped no one else in the building heard it. “Give it to Eileen. Thank you, and sleep well.”

I didn’t mean to upset her but I didn’t want to wait around for a discourse on my profession. She had been like a mother to me ever since I got back from the war. She would have done her best to dissuade me from whatever foolish thing I planned.

There was no guarantee this flimsy set of conclusions would protect me but I was certain neither Mrs. Morgan-Smith nor Liam Smathers wanted to take any chances. On the other hand, the sense of desperation associated with years of hiding was the eventual crop sown from their wickedness. They might have been ready to harvest with one mighty swing of a scythe.

Chapter Twelve

I was grateful both of the cats allowed me to sleep in. The prior day was long and tedious, grueling from both a mental and emotional standpoint, not to mention the excessive amount of driving. Dredging through the past was akin to digging up a grave. In most cases, it would have been prudent to leave well enough alone and let the dead sleep as peacefully as they could. Unfortunately, I was hired by Slyvia Morgan-Smith and set upon this path by her. As usually happens, all roads return to the same point of origin. A circle will always come complete.

It was my intention to check on Art Stover. While I was not beholden to him for anything remotely resembling professional courtesy, common human decency did push me in that direction. On top of which he passed out from a brutal beating on my doorstep. Yet, at this moment, I knew I required some sage guidance. For most Jews, that meant turning to their rabbi. For me, it was my father.

The little shop on the corner of South Kansas Avenue and East Douglas Avenue could not have been more obscure if it wanted to be. It was, however, within proximity to both the temple and my father's house. Officially, or at least according to the sign on the window, the establishment was a watch and clock repairman. My father had additional skills with regard to jewelry, metallurgy, and knowledge of all kinds of antiques. He still made enough of a living to be well-fed and have the freedom to read the Bible and study the Talmud as it suited his needs. He found the balance in life that I still sought.

Attached to his glasses were a pair of magnifying lenses that allowed for the detailed work of his profession. Initially, whenever anyone entered the store, he needed a moment to adjust his vision from the extremely close to the remotely distant. After several seconds, a welcoming smile greeted me.

"And to what do I owe the pleasure of this visit?" he asked.

"Can't a son visit his father for no specific purpose?"

"Most sons, yes." My father knew me well. He probably got his sense of humor from Fanny Brice.

I left my face blank for a moment. I was uncertain as to what to ask without it being a direct reflection of the case I worked on. What did I have a need to know? What was the deeper meaning, the purpose of the inquiry?

"How important is the past?" I didn't direct the question to him, per se, or even consider a significant event or piece of the past. I was far too general for a viable answer. As always, my father surprised me.

"I will never forget the first time I met your mother or the day you were born. I often think of your mother's passing and sitting *shiva* with members of the temple and at the same time being proud of what you were doing, fighting for your country. But I also know I focus on today. This moment." He held a pocket watch. "This trinket that someone has entrusted me to restore.

Remember Isaiah."

When I returned from the war, damaged and beaten by the weary years and the toll of needing to kill other men to preserve freedom, I often could not sleep because of all that occurred. In two separate instances, both Rabbi Saperstein and my father referenced Isaiah 43:18-19.

Remember ye not the former things, neither consider the things of old./Behold I will do a new thing; now it shall spring forth; shall ye not know it? I will even make a way in the wilderness, and rivers in the desert.

The past eight or nine months were my efforts to move forward and not cling to the past. Why was it I could not let someone else do the same thing? Then it finally dawned on me that Sylvia Morgan-Smith and Liam Smathers intentionally buried the past as they eliminated all who knew of it and wouldn't allow it to fade away into obscurity. They buried it forcefully, kicking and screaming. I had no proof of the murders of Chubb McFarland, Billy Fintelman and his wife, or any of the others. This wasn't merely a case of allowing an old woman to live out her days in peace. These were cold and calculated measures that required justice. Art Stover had an opportunity for redemption. I hoped he would take it.

It didn't appear that way initially. After I got permission from the nurse to visit, I walked in to find a stubborn pig-headed man bandaged in several places, primarily around his face and torso. He was hooked to an IV and lay completely still in his bed. His primary movement was to jerk his head away and stare at the wall after I entered, and he recognized me.

"Looks like you're not going to be bowling any time soon." My attempt at humor fell on deaf ears. I had a feeling nothing I said would have penetrated the brick wall he constructed. I had to convince him I was not the enemy.

"Go away."

"No," I said sharply.

He turned suddenly, a mix of anger, disappointment, and frustration peering from behind his eyes.

My guess was he took a chance and failed. The opportunity for a big payout fell flat and he would wind up again a two-bit penny ante player in a world of the rich and powerful, barely able to scrape up enough for a daily meal. Only someone like me in the same profession would recognize what he considered failure.

"What do you want, Bergman? I got zip for my efforts except bruises and contusions and a whopping headache."

"You ever been worked over like that before?"

"Never." At that moment, I touched a nerve that brought out his sense of pride.

"Smathers is good, isn't he?"

"Pendergast hires the best."

That caught me off guard. Until then, I figured Sylvia Morgan-Smith had extricated herself from the Kansas City machine shortly after her husband died. My information led me to believe she left after Pendergast paid her off handsomely when she turned over documents and files that would have been an embarrassment to a lot of politicos. The assumption I made was Liam Smathers was somehow connected to the old Eddie Adams gang and the former Sally Minter would be more comfortable with someone of that ilk.

"You're not making sense," I responded.

Art Stover smiled slowly, as though he were infused

with more than blood. New life flowed through him now. He considered it the upper hand.

"Big twists and turns, huh, Bergman? Like a Coney Island roller coaster."

"Spill."

"Why?"

"Because you've got nothing left. It's going to take you quite a while to recover from this. You know you can't handle Smathers any other way than sneaking up behind him and putting a bullet in his brain. If you're lucky enough to get close."

"What makes you so different? What makes you so special?"

"I'm not. But I'm smarter."

Stover sank into morose silence after I punctured the balloon of his bravado. He simply stared at me while the words chiseled away through that brick wall. This wasn't a soldier in a theater of war who realized his wounds would ultimately cause his death. This was an unscrupulous man who finally understood he didn't have a leg to stand on and had been defeated at the only game he knew how to play. It held no honor.

A big deep exhale followed a bigger and deeper breath. Then the story unfolded. Chubb McFarland reached out to Stover with an explosive piece of information. But McFarland met his demise and Stover didn't believe the robbery angle in light of what was about to happen. Stover made overtures to his contacts in the police department, learned about McFarland's connection to Eddie Adams and then started to look up other gang members and hangers-on. He knew D.C. Brown from his days when he was on the other side of the law and learned Pendergast made sure Sylvia

Morgan-Smith was followed to ensure her silence regarding all things associated with the machine. Somewhere along the way, Pendergast's motivations and intentions changed, likely around the time he served a stretch in Leavenworth in 1939.

At this point it was difficult to determine if the lady directed these activities or Smathers had ulterior motives and acted on his own behalf. Stover tried to worm his way in, get close to Mrs. Morgan-Smith, and insinuate he had information that was detrimental to her standing. All he had was innuendo but it was enough for him to back away when it appeared Smathers was on to him.

"Did Smathers kill Georgette Finster?"

"That would be my guess."

"What about Jessie Clarkson? Where is she now?"

"Don't know. Went up to see her in Newton. Tried to get her to come back with me. You know, use her as leverage to squeeze some cabbage out of the old lady. She wasn't in that rundown rat trap. On the way back, I was tailed. Tried to shake him but he finally got to me."

"And that is when you stumbled into my apartment?"

"I had every mind to tell you what was going on but, you know, I passed out."

"You could have told me sooner."

"Hey, a guy's gotta make a buck, right? How was I gonna eat?"

It was a valid argument but as far as I knew the dead don't have much of an appetite.

I was uncertain as to how to proceed. This could all be over if I simply dropped the matter. Then I pondered that I might be considered too dangerous for either the lady or the tiger as I learned a great deal more than they thought I would. Just like a soldier who wore a uniform, I still had a target on my back. After seeing the results of Stover's encounter, I understood the degree of difficulty.

However, I had little concrete evidence to present to the police either as a citizen and especially as a former police officer. Everything made sense and actually added up. But nothing was substantial enough to put before a district attorney. It would make a great story for a writer.

I started to leave but Stover grabbed my arm.

"You need to talk to a lawyer named Christopher Smithson. He works out of his home. Ten Thirty-Eight West Riverside."

"What for?"

"The old lady told me he drew up her will."

"What makes you think he'll talk to me? They have bigger issues with client privilege than detectives do."

"You tell him what you know, and he'll do what he can to protect his client."

"From what?"

"Getting bumped off."

Stover appeared to collapse even though he was still awake. He used every bit of energy he had to give me what he knew. There was a recognition of defeat. I was likely to be his champion, the one to see this through to the end. As I saw it that end could be winding up in a hospital bed or a coffin.

Christopher Smithson initially thought I was a perspective client. He had a finely trimmed all white goatee and smooth combed back snow white hair. For a man who worked out of his home, he still dressed in a three-piece dark blue suit with a gray shirt and a dark blue and green tartan tie with a gold stick pin. His shoes were highly polished, almost to the extent of what I remembered from the military. He was well past his sixties but his firm handshake indicated he did not live a dissipated lifestyle.

"After all my years working downtown, I found it more restful to maintain a small office in my home," he explained. "My clients are few though very loyal." There was a pleasant pause before he continued. "And how may I assist you, Mr. Bergman?"

"We share a common client. Mrs. Sylvia Morgan-Smith."

His self-assurance took a hit like a boxer who was stung by an unexpected jab.

"Oh," was all he could respond.

I smiled and waited to see if he would expand upon his exclamation. He recovered his breath and pulled his shoulders back.

"Long story short is that she hired me to find a gentleman who had become her confidante. Well, I found him, or rather he found me. He stumbled into my apartment after receiving a vicious beating from who we believe is Liam Smathers." I conveniently forgot to include all the historical details which I presumed Mr. Smithson was completely acquainted with. My hope was he believed I knew nothing more.

"How awful." The comment lacked empathy and emotion. It was a statement more than a compassionate observation, merely some blather to say to fill in the gaps. Art Stover received no consideration from Christopher Smithson.

We stared at each other and waited. From both his profession and age, I was aware he had more practice at this than I did. I hoped strength of character would help me be more successful because it was all I had.

"Mr. Bergman, you understand the strict nature of attorney-client privilege and how this must be maintained at all costs," he finally continued as though about to deliver a summation.

"Perfectly."

"Assuming, for a moment, a client wished to make a personal decision that her attorney decided was not in her best interests, the attorney would, naturally, make a case, so to speak, to adjust this course of action. My job, as you can imagine, is not to say 'no' arbitrarily but to offer alternatives that would be more suitable. Everything in the best interests of the client."

As he played the supposition game, I helped him continue.

"Well, could you present a hypothetical example? Just for clarity's sake."

"Let us say an elderly woman wishes to make changes to a final will and testament. Perhaps something along the lines of who she would bequeath substantial holdings to. The disposition of her estate, as it were. And if, hypothetically of course, the benefactor would be the type of person to facilitate this process earlier than the Laws of Nature would normally dictate, the attorney might present cautionary advice to the contrary."

My encounters with lawyers were few and far between. I understood why. It occurred to me they were cut from the same cloth as bankers.

"Doesn't every client, in fact every individual, have the right to dispose of their estate as they see fit? What is in, as you have stated, their best interests?"

"Theoretically that is true. However, some examples are more, shall we say bluntly, suicidal than others."

"Perhaps that is the underlying motivation."

As soon as I said it, everything became clear. It seemed even Mr. Christopher Smithson, Esq. felt the same. The past can often dictate the future, in spite of what a passage from the book of Isaiah may say otherwise.

Chapter Thirteen

I drove to 1210 North Emporia with a sense of urgency but made sure not to break any traffic laws. What I was able to infer turned out to be perhaps a moralistic sense of self-retribution. I could not initially believe someone as calculating as Sylvia Morgan-Smith would deliberately make an effort to bring about her own demise. Perhaps the past had caught up with her in the presence of Art Stover. Maybe the slightest bit of guilt permeated her tough exterior after so many years of hiding from the ghosts. She might just be tired and yearned for the frivolity of the 1920s or the stature of the 1930s. Either way my aim was to get her to divulge the truth, if only for my sense of righteousness.

Strangely, the front door was unlocked. No car in the driveway and the open garage door indicated no one but the lady of the house was at home. If that. As it turned out, I found her in the parlor where we first met. She sat upright as though she were at the head of a receiving line. Her eyes were fixed on me the moment I entered.

"You look like a man who has the weight of the world on his shoulders," she declared with the kind of bitterness reserved for the wealthy and privileged. She resented me or perhaps the dignity of my morals.

"Not more than you, madame."

"You stand there with your conjectures, the stories you have gleaned of the past, and you presume to know who I am now based on who I was then? Tsk, tsk. How uncouth. Isn't there something in your faith about judgment, Mr. Bergman?"

"Leviticus. Chapter 19. Verse 15. *Ye shall do no unrighteousness in judgment: thou shalt not respect the person of the poor, nor honor the person of the mighty: but in righteousness shalt thou judge thy neighbor.*"

I stood there, our eyes fixed on each other, she with her indignation that someone so beneath her should press for answers from a mere twenty-five years prior, and me with a sense of justice instilled by a religion well over five thousand years old. As far as I was concerned, I had time on my side.

"There will be no confessions here today, Mr. Bergman. I've lived my life as I have seen fit and will see to my end in the same manner."

"Did you instruct Liam Smathers to kill all those people?" I asked, almost ignoring her declaration.

"No." The word dropped like the bombs on Japan. "Anyone who knew of me who could be a threat to the Kansas City machine needed to be eliminated. Smathers was on orders from Pendergast."

Even in death, Thomas Pendergast exerted a great influence. His legacy was already tainted. By three months, he missed witnessing his protégé ascend to the presidency. The power of evil can be greater than we can imagine.

"But then Stover comes along and references Georgette Finster and Jessie Clarkson."

"Yes."

"And they were a new threat."

"Yes. They were young flappers. Cheap young good-time girls. Inconsequential really. But they saw enough and heard enough to cause trouble if they wanted to. If it came to money, they would certainly want to."

"I know about Finster. What happened to Clarkson?" She looked away for a moment. That was all the answer I needed. "Stover is still alive. He's in the hospital being guarded by the police. He'll talk."

"I know."

Sally Minter walked away with a lot of dough in 1921, got as far as Kansas City, and bought her way in to high society. The problem was she didn't realize her dilapidated husband was tied in with a corrupt political boss who would do whatever it took to hold on to his power. When her husband died, she had no further leverage and had to run away yet again. This time she was saddled with a gorilla named Liam Smathers. Chauffeur, house boy, and enforcer. Sylvia Morgan-Smith was not accepted into the upper echelon of Wichita. Perhaps someone recognized she lacked the true sophistication required. For the last fifteen years, she was a faded chickadee in a gilded cage who endured all the killings that she believed were required.

Now, with Pendergast dead, none of that really mattered. Perhaps Smathers figured he was owed compensation for the expenditure of time and effort. Whatever pressure he placed upon her, physical or emotional, her will was changed to make him the sole beneficiary. Now, the only way he could collect would be by her passing.

"So, how does it end?" I asked.

"You tell me. Perhaps it is all for the best."

At that moment, I was completely incredulous. The sense of selfish entitlement filled the room like a cheap perfume. She exuded not an iota of remorse. She lived her life with no regrets.

"You may be done with your life, lady. You might have figured it was a good run and now it's time for it to end. Just remember Art Stover is out there and he knows quite a bit. As do I. You may be okay with Smathers covering your face with a pillow one night while you recline on satin sheets. But this won't be over after you're gone. Smathers will still be looking over his shoulder just the way you have been. And he won't feel safe until all the demons have been exorcised."

"And what will that matter to me?"

The callousness showed she had always been a cold and calculating woman. She might actually have been the one to egg on Eddie Adams who, until then, had been a two-bit punk. What caused him to become a raving madman? The race was almost over, and the tired nag would be put out to pasture.

Naturally, I left out any mention of Eileen and the document I placed in Mrs. Hanover's care. Yet I still had to be concerned. Smathers was not one to be disregarded as simply a brute. He traveled to Texas, Oklahoma, Missouri, and then to Kansas City over the years to carry out a series of what could only be called executions. To my knowledge there was no evidence in these cases that would tie in to him. I did not know the full extent of the lady's estate but I guessed it would keep Smathers comfortable for the rest of his life. Yet, I realized the greater adversary did not seem to be around.

"Where's Smathers?" I demanded.

"I don't know." She stared straight at me and did not so much as bother to look around in even the faintest attempt to consider my inquiry.

"Where is he?"

“I don’t know,” she retorted with equal force.

“I’ll just wait for him.”

“He wouldn’t be foolish enough to confront you here, especially with your car out front.”

“I could hide it in your garage.”

“You fool! He could be watching you now.”

I had no response. It was a parry and riposte that left me with nothing further to attack. I could feel my foot throb from the frustration of the encounter. It was both a barometer for weather and danger.

“I’m not about to let him come here and end your life because you’re tired of it.” My tone became clipped and forced.

“And what about your life, Mr. Bergman? Is it a worthy price to pay to kick up the dust from a sordid past? Dredge up stories that even the police have no further interest in?”

“Mrs. Morgan-Smith, is your life worth the price to pay for the iniquities of the past?”

“Yes, it is. One way or another.”

She had a point in one regard. If she were arrested and brought to trial, she would likely have been sentenced to prison. As such, her life would be forfeit to the state. She opted instead to end it by accepting her murder as a form of execution. She was her own judge and jury. She simply chose a different executioner. I could understand it all to a degree. Nevertheless, I was certain Liam Smathers did not have the same sensibility or honor. He would not stop until his work was done. Completely and efficiently.

I stood on the porch and tried to figure out how to protect my former client while I brought Smathers to the attention of the police. I saw the fabulous car that I first encountered on a picnic with Eileen while we were at Park Villa. That fairy tale seemed ages ago; it was merely five days. The car sat just south of Eleventh Street parked on the opposite side. I couldn't be sure if he wanted to be discreet or really didn't care anymore. He would either wait until I left and finish business here, or follow me knowing an older lady could be attended to at any time. I put it to the test.

I pulled away slowly from the curb and continued north on the one-way street. In my mirror, I saw the car follow me, slowly but close enough. Now, I had to figure where I could go to lure this beast.

I would not have the opportunity to stop into a drug store and make a phone call, even if I knew who to call. I couldn't draw him downtown or put King Mar and his staff in jeopardy. Alonzo Washington went back to work at Cudahy but there was no place there that could be useful. It was then I thought of Sibyl, the blind colored lady who had a deep hand in a criminal element who actually tried to protect Alonzo before they determined I acted in his best interests. I hoped the run-down house on Old Lawrence Road was still used by them. Otherwise, it would be a lonely place to die.

At Seventeenth Street, I turned west until I got to Broadway. I continued north before I reached Thirty-Seventh Street, made a quick right and then a sharp left. The classy vehicle did not enjoy the railroad tracks as much as my noble Sir Pounce-mobile. The first time I was brought to this house, I was blindfolded. I still remembered how to get back.

I parked in front and made sure Smathers knew this was where I stopped. I stepped out of the car and said a little prayer before I went into the house. That rickety wooden dining room table with two chairs, the wobbly rocking chair, and further dust and distant memories occupied the place like reluctant tenants. Unfortunately for me, there were no real people. This would be where the showdown took place. Me with my wits and experience and he with whatever he needed beyond brute strength.

The door opened and the brightness from a mid-July afternoon poured in. It looked more like the light from Heaven than what you would find at the state fair. The hulking mound of man stood in the doorway and blocked out the warmth. Neither of us moved.

"Funny place you pick," he said contemptuously.

"For what?"

"To die."

"Oh, that. Don't you know by now, Smathers, the past always catches up to you? Someone knows you. Maybe even from the Pendergast gang. You think you're cleaning up a mess? You're just creating a new one."

I had no idea what his actual intentions were, but he took a step forward. There was precious little time to consider what to do next. Suddenly, a voice came from outside.

"Bergman, is that you?"

I recognized the scratchy voice of a woman who surprised me with her awareness, control, and power. I never knew how old Sybil was. I never needed to know. She stepped into the room with her tall lanky son Jason behind her. Sybil held a cane; Jason, a gun.

"You never used a cane before, Sybil."

"Had a bit of a fall a little while ago. Just using it till I get my sense of balance back." We were like two old friends. Perhaps we were. "Jason and me was coming here to clean up a spell when he saw one fine looking car headed here. You moving up in the world?"

"No, ma'am. That one belongs to Mr. Liam Smathers here."

Her movements included a twitch of her eyebrow, a turn of her head to lean an ear closer, and what appeared to be a sniffing action of her nose. She sized up the man in the best way she knew how. In all my years, I never knew a policeman who could do better.

"Friend of yours?"

"Oh, not quite."

"What you want us to do with him?"

"Keep him comfortable for a bit until I can get someone here to collect him."

"Now you know I don't cotton much to the police, Mr. Bergman. We don't see eye to eye, so to speak." She laughed at her own joke.

"Yes, ma'am. Well, it will just be one and I'll make him promise to close his eyes."

She smiled. I guessed she could sense my smile.

****

I fetched Clarence Mendenhall just as he came on duty and encouraged him to follow me. Strangely, neither Sybil nor Jason was there when we got back about forty-five minutes later. Liam Smathers, however, was tied and gagged to the rocking chair. In his efforts to extricate himself, he had toppled over. Mendenhall agreed to have him taken in while he consulted with the jurisdictions of the places where Smathers was presumed to have committed other crimes and to check on outstanding warrants. The case was by no means over but at least Art Stover, Eileen, and myself were safe for now, as well as Sylvia Morgan-Smith.

I returned to her home to discuss what happened. A thought in my head from my days in the police department whispered there was no real crime she was guilty of. Absconding with money from armed robberies could not be proven, especially if that money had been laundered through a legitimate bank and so many years ago at that. She would likely have alibis for the other murders that could be verified. There were only the salacious aspects of the past that created the greatest guilt.

She sat in the same chair. Neither a prideful look nor one of defiance showed on her face. Her head was slumped in her chest, one hand in her lap, the other dangling off to the side. An empty wine glass was on its side on a small mahogany table next to her. My two fingers went to her neck to search for a pulse but came away unsuccessful. I leaned toward the table. A deep fragrance of bitter almonds, the kind of decay that permeates a life that had been wasted, took hold. Sylvia Morgan-Smith decided not to waste any more time.

Chapter Fourteen

What I needed at that moment was the familiar and comfortable, a way to remind me of the here and now, and would not drag me back kicking and screaming to the past, like the war or the Whitmans or the Nathans. The Pan American Café was the only place worthwhile at the moment. It held the kind of warmth that would send the shivers of despair away.

King Mar's smile evaporated like the morning mist on a warm summer's day when I entered. From our long acquaintance, he knew something was amiss to the extent his mere presence was all that was needed. I got an order of chicken fried rice and two egg rolls and ate them lazily, not really succeeding in my endeavor to forget the distraction this case caused me.

Albert Whitman hired me. He was killed because of his malfeasance. Sylvia Morgan-Smith hired me. She took her life because of guilt over her indiscretions. I tried to make a clear distinction between these two. Their common bond of deceased former clients gave me grave doubts about what I actually accomplished.

For a moment, I reminisced on my own past. There was nothing in my childhood to be ashamed of or cause regrets. I excelled in my duties as a policeman. I survived the war with but a bad ankle and a limp to go with the memories of the horrors that men could perpetrate on each other. My mother passed away. It was, however, my abiding desire to understand humanity, and by extension, myself, that I became a private detective. Now was not the time to regret that decision, merely because of what I had encountered thus far. There is often pain in the realization of the workings of mankind. Truth comes with a heavy price.

The only other peace I would find would be from two felines who required attention and love. My first obligation was to attend to their bellies. I hung my jacket, rolled up my sleeves, and took off my shoes while they ate. Afterward, they both jumped on the sofa to sit with me and eagerly fought for my attention. The simplicity of rubbing an ear or a belly resulted in purrs of satisfaction. It was a validation that I could do a *mitzvah* for one of the Lord's creatures on this earth. It provided a momentary sense of satisfaction. To my knowledge, they slept on either side of me that night.

All three of us had a full breakfast the next morning. Clarnece Mendenhall asked me to come to the station to file a formal complaint against Liam Smathers and provide as much detailed information as I could in order to assist with the investigations in other states. Before I left, I retrieved the documents from Mrs. Hanover who was thoroughly relieved to have them returned to me. She spoke no further about it. To do so would have distressed her.

It appeared rather busy for a late Friday morning in the middle of July. I witnessed Mendenhall go back and forth between two offices that were side by side as I waited in one of the chairs in front of the desk sergeant's station. Mendenhall looked harried, not the tired fatigue of investigating a horrible murder but more to do with the frustrations associated with bureaucracy. I recognized the signs. While I had thoughts of joining the Night Detective Squad, this aspect of police work squashed those notions just as quickly.

Eventually, a uniformed officer escorted Liam Smathers from one of the offices. Mendenhall came out behind them and stood in the lobby as Smathers left on his own recognizance.

"I'll fill you in," Mendenhall said to me directly, anticipating my query. "Follow me."

We went into the other office. Comfortably ensconced in one of the better chairs was Christopher Smithson, Esq., immaculately dressed as though on his way to a polo match, and Art Stover, dressed in a new suit that seemed to conflict with the bandages on his face and one of his hands. These were two of the strangest bedfellows I could imagine. Just like attending the matinee, I waited for the curtain to rise. This promised to be quite a show.

"The death of Sylvia Morgan-Smith has been ruled as a suicide," Mendenhall read from an official report. "This department is satisfied that no outside suspicious forces acted upon her. Mr. Smathers has presented eyewitnesses to corroborate his whereabouts when other murders had taken place in various other jurisdictions. We will be passing that information to the respective agencies in those states. Mr. Smathers has, however, been charged with five counts of theft and three motor violations. He has made restitution on the former and will appear in court early next week for what will likely be a substantial fine."

Mendenhall closed the folder and sat there. The police portion of this entertainment program obviously ended. Now we would get to the lawyer part. That was where there would be more words of greater eloquence and obsequiousness. It would give Shakespeare a run for his money. I waited as patiently as I could.

"Mr. Smathers had no undue cause to harm his employer," the honorable Mr. Smithson announced. I took unspoken umbrage with the description of Smathers as an employee, now aware he was thrust upon her by greater forces. "Mr. Stover is to receive the bulk of Mrs. Morgan-Smith's estate. Naturally, there will be a formal reading of the will, but I considered it prudent to advise Detective Mendenhall so as to not place any further burden upon Mr. Smathers when it certainly was not warranted. In my opinion, of course."

"I don't get it," I said. I was tired of the formal verbiage from both sides and wanted a little plain speaking. Art Stover looked more than capable. In his opinion, of course. After a glance at what was now his attorney, he could speak freely.

"Look, I went there initially to put the bite on the lady. Chubb McFarland was a three-time loser. I knew about him from before."

"Oh really," I said with a bored disbelief. He ignored me.

"But, you know, after spending time with her, I got to see she was nothing less than a scared dame who was looking for a friend."

A snort and a gasp were what passed for my disbelief.

"And you, of all people, were her friend?"

"Okay, Bergman, I'm no Father Flanagan. But the old gal got to me. I promised her I'd find some dirt on Smathers to help get rid of him. Turns out he was trying to get rid of me. And I didn't know nothin' about this will until Mr. Smithson here came to the hospital yesterday."

It would have been insulting if he swore to that on the proverbial stack of bibles. I turned toward Smithson and thought for the briefest of moments I might have been able to trip him up.

"With regard to that, Mr. Smithson, you led me to believe Mrs. Morgan-Smith was making a mistake in regard to changes in her will. I assumed you were referring to Smathers."

"To be perfectly honest, Mr. Bergman," he began as though he rehearsed a summation, "I had doubts about Mr. Stover's character as well. Then again, he had no association with a political machine and acted solely as an *illibata persona.* My feeling was she should donate her estate to a worthwhile charity as a kind of, well, absolution. While I still believe that would have been a more judicious choice, at this time, I can find no fault with the current resolution."

My Latin was rusty but to refer to Stover as an "unblemished" or "innocent" person in this matter pushed the bounds of truth to the extreme. I had to give credit to Smithson for his skills. Stover would have a lot to live up to.

That, as they say, was that. The police literally closed their file, and the probate courts were ready to do likewise. Perhaps the wheels of justice came full circle twenty-five years later. At this point, it was not for me to say.

I had a thought of consulting with Mendenhall or, for that matter, reaching out to Smathers. In the end, I simply waited for Smithson to be done with his new client and approached Stover on the steps outside.

"You're a smart guy, Stover."

"I'd like to think I am." A self-satisfied smile appeared on his face.

"The police would have come up with something on Smathers."

"You know that ain't so. Too far in the past, Bergman. It's old news. Nobody cares."

"Yeah, but now Smathers is free with just a slap on the wrist. I'll just bet he is real sore about not landing that pot of gold he'd been waiting on all these years. And, if I had a dollar, I'd bet he'll hold you responsible." I leaned in close, to make absolutely sure he understood me. "I'd watch my back, Art. I don't think you'll be enjoying that nest egg for as long as you think."

I patted him on the shoulder and walked away and enjoyed the late morning sun as it revived my spirits. I reminded myself there is more than the police or the courts to dole out justice. That notion rejuvenated me.

The rest of the day was spent in leisure. I drove around, went to a few stores to peruse the trinkets and unnecessary merchandise, and finally wound up outside the Beacon Building when Eileen got done with work.

"This is a surprise," she declared rather plainly.

"Is it a pleasant surprise?"

"It is."

"Let's swing by your place so you can get changed for a date."

"Anything fancy?"

"Burgers at Candyland and a movie."

She had a look of impressed satisfaction. I waited in the car while she changed into a linen blouse and skirt but with comfortable shoes. The burgers were thick and juicy. The malteds were rich. We acted like a couple of silly teenagers. A Charlie Chan flick, *Shadows Over Chinatown*, played along with the typical newsreel and cartoon. The movie starred Sydney Toler who actually grew up in Wichita. I bought popcorn and Junior Mints and almost made myself sick after I had stuffed my gullet at dinner.

It was a beautiful evening, so we took the liberty of a stroll down Broadway toward Douglas Avenue. Eileen kept glancing over at me. She obviously noticed the broad smile I did not feel compelled to hide.

"Harold Bergman, what is up with you?"

"I just realized it is not for me to judge but to live in the service of the Most High."

"It took the burger, the malted, and all that candy and popcorn to come to that conclusion?"

I stopped dead in my tracks, turned to her, and held her hands in mine.

"Come to think of it we were interrupted in the park last Saturday," I declared.

"And?"

"Tomorrow is Saturday."

"And?"

"This time we'll have a real picnic."

I leaned in and kissed her, right on the corner of Broadway and Douglas Avenue. There was no need to think about the past. I focused on the future.

Chapter Fifteen

Unfortunately, the future had to be put on hold as something came up. Mrs. Hanover thought she saw someone peer into her window in a suspicious fashion. I spent most of that Saturday evening on a good old-fashioned stakeout in her apartment, fell asleep in an uncomfortable thick wooden chair that looked out her kitchen window, and woke on Sunday morning with a stiff neck and sore back. I checked outside and found no evidence of an intruder. No footprints in the dirt or attempted shimmy of the window She apologized profusely but I made sure she knew it was of no consequence to me. I owed her a great deal more than she could ever realize. I did, however, borrow her phone to advise Eileen of the circumstances and to indicate I would need proper sleep in a real bed. Mrs. Hanover offered me breakfast, but I politely declined.

As it turned out, a couple more weeks passed and we never got around to our picnic. This was largely due to my own growing apprehensions as time allowed me to contemplate further. I realized there is a stark contrast between adhering to the age-old traditions of your religion and being stuck in the past. While I was not a rabbi as my father would have preferred, I was a devout Jew, beholden to the moral dictates found in the Laws. Yet the moral nuances from my former profession as a police officer coupled with my experiences in the theaters of war kept me from reaching forward into what would resemble a more fulfilled future.

I witnessed the impact such a grip held on the late Sylvia Morgan-Smith. Even though she escaped from the clutches of her criminal associations and found a stepping stone to a more appropriate social circle, she was entrapped by events twenty-five years behind her. I knew for certain I did not want to wind up like her.

It was clear I needed to make a choice between a resolution of my undefined concerns with life and humanity or continuing to foster a relationship and possibly a family with Eileen. For the former, I could keep on with my current occupation. For the latter, I would need a viable job. A return to the police force would not have been advisable. Then again, I truly had no other skills. Where could one be an investigator or researcher and still work in an office Monday through Friday? Then it dawned on me, and I made a plan of action.

I put on a clean shirt, a freshly pressed pair of pants, and tie, polished my shoes and drove to the Farmers and Bankers Life Insurance building. It was late afternoon on Friday, August 2nd. I didn't want to catch them at closing at the end of the week nor did I feel it was prudent to make an appointment which they might have declined. This was to be what salesmen referred to as a "cold call." I never worked as a salesman, so this was all new to me.

Troy Harding spoke with the receptionist as I walked in. He saw me, raised one eyebrow, and then faced me with his arms crossed. He had no idea why I was there but did his best to present a front of control and stability.

"Mr. Bergman, how may we assist you?"

“I understand you may have an opening here.”

That caught him completely off guard. I hadn’t checked the newspapers but was certain they placed no employment ad there. He knew that as well. Curiosity must have gotten the better of him. He checked with the receptionist and confirmed he had no appointments for the rest of the day, then invited me into his office. The last time I was there I was handed a check for one thousand two-hundred and fifty dollars. I did not expect to be that fortunate once again. I would have better luck at some church’s Bingo night.

Harding nodded with his hands folded on the top of his desk. I made the play, so he offered me the chance to go first.

“I’m not exactly sure the specific nature of the position Kelly Gardner held but I can assure you I am equal to the task and more.”

“To be perfectly frank,” Harding started after clearing his throat loudly, “Kelly Gardner used his legal acumen to find loopholes in policies to allow us to avoid paying on claims of a dubious nature. To some, that may sound crude. But it is the nature of the business.”

“That didn’t seem to work too well with Sharon Kaye though.”

“No. It didn’t.” His tone was one of retreat.

“And yet I was able to save your firm from a rather sizeable payout.”

“True.” He appeared to swallow very hard to say that simple word. From a military perspective, this was a frontal assault via a surprise attack.

“There are just as many ways someone with my abilities can address these spurious concerns. I was a police officer and still have connections within the force.

I am well known in the community and highly trusted by diverse segments of the population. As for the legal aspects, let's just say I am acquainted with a few lawyers who might point me in the right direction should such be required."

"What exactly are you suggesting, Mr. Bergman?"

"Being on permanent retainer with Farmers and Bankers Life Insurance. A modest salary. Reimbursement of expenses. And a percentage of any recovery, similar to the Kaye life insurance policy."

He stared at me for a moment and blinked his eyes. I couldn't tell precisely what went through his head. I guessed no one had ever approached him in such a fashion in his many years in this business. He called for Thomas Van Sickle on the intercom. As was typical, Van Sickle entered with his shirt sleeves rolled up. I recalled he oversaw the adjusters and would likely be the one to approve this position, were it required actual approval.

Harding went over my recitation, and I occasionally corrected or amended his comments. It was Van sickle who had a pleasantly surprised look on his face as though someone recommended a new restaurant in town or place for a summer vacation. They asked me to wait in the front office. At the very least, they didn't kick me out thoughtlessly. I considered that a plus.

It was about four thirty. I imagined they would bide their time, call me in to thank me for the intriguing offer, and then respectfully decline. It was less than five minutes later when they called me back.

"We created the position for Kelly Gardner," Van Sickle began, "out of a sense of Christian charity. He had been an excellent lawyer at one point before allowing drink to overcome him."

I wondered if I was in the presence of insurance men or missionaries.

"Our adjusters are largely fact gatherers," Van Sickle continued. "Gardner had the intellectual capacity to assimilate the data and make a wide variety of determinations."

"Your offer, Mr. Bergman, based on your many years of experience, would allow us to replace Kelly Gardner's position as well as eliminate a couple of our adjusters. In essence, you could be both a fact gatherer and analyst." Harding settled into his role as 'boss of the office' quite comfortably.

Van Sickle picked it up. "This would mean we could create a hybrid position for you that, well, no other insurance agency has at this moment. You'd be helping us emerge into the forefront of this industry. As far as the adjuster positions go."

"I would like to say, however," Harding said softly, like an English butler, "that the previous recovery percentage you, um, negotiated with us would not be manageable from a fiscal standpoint."

In essence, they agreed to my offer yet still tried to figure how they could come out ahead in the bottom line. Right then and there, we made an appointment for first thing on Monday morning to finalize the new position, outline its parameters, and negotiate all manner of compensation. For the first time since I applied to the police academy, I felt like I took steps toward getting a real job.

This was only a first step. This was not the time to celebrate. If this could be an occupation I could transition into, I would be in a position to offer a sound and solid life to Eileen. It was to be a quiet weekend with the cats and maybe a dinner at the Pan American.

I re-read *I and Thou* by Martin Buber, then finally got around to *The Lady in the Lake* by Raymond Chandler. From Buber, I tried to determine how our existence has meaning through relationships but was torn between seeking a deeper one with the Almighty and fostering one with Eileen. I previously resisted reading any of the so-called hardboiled writers for fear I would not measure up to a fictional standard. Chandler's writing was crisp and sassy. I knew, though, that I wasn't Philip Marlowe nor would ever be. Then again, Marlowe would have a difficult time being me.

Monday rolled around. I regressed to the feelings of a six-year old on the first day of school. I prepared myself for some orientation on the industry followed by whatever degree of a case load to manage. Instead, I encountered what amounted to an audition.

"We've spoken to the owners of the agency," Troy Harding said.

I wondered when that occurred as I visited with them late on Friday and now it was eight in the morning on Monday.

"The kind of restructuring would be an investment of time and money, and we want to minimize the risk. After all, that is the business we're in."

Both he and Tom Van Sickle chuckled at the inside joke. When it was apparent I was not in on the humor, Van Sickle proceeded.

"Are you familiar with Glen Hubbell?"

"Rich guy in Eastborough. Made his money through real estate if what I heard is correct."

"It is. He bought a lot of property prior to the war from folks who were about to go into foreclosure and then either sold to the government or developed communities for people who could afford his type of housing. He is, in a word, unscrupulous."

"But you do business with him."

"If we don't, someone else will," Harding chimed in.

"We currently have a claim from him for a stolen necklace valued at nearly twenty-five hundred dollars," Van sickle continued. "A police report was filed but as of late, there is no resolution or pending arrest. We have a limited amount of time before we must resolve the claim."

"We figure with your investigative skills as well as your, shall we say, acquaintance with the police, you might be able to save this company a sizable amount." Harding treated me like a piece of toast as he buttered me up.

I looked back and forth between them and waited for the rest of the commentary. The part where they tell me how much this job is worth. The silence gave way to an embarrassed response.

"We've decided on a daily fee of fifteen dollars, all reasonable expenses to be reimbursed and two percent of recovery." Harding appeared proud of himself.

"On the Kaye life insurance policy, you indicated three percent."

"Yes, we did. But as this is a trial run, so to speak—"

"Gentlemen," I said, my hand raised like a traffic cop, "while I appreciate your wanting to ensure this relationship will be satisfactory, I cannot enter into employment with a company who does not issue forth a sense of trust with their employees. Why don't we just talk straight so we can have a fruitful relationship?"

Harding sat. That was the signal for Van Sickle to sit. I tried to be one of the guys and sat as well.

"We are going to be releasing two adjusters in order to take you on in this position. If we have to upend a man's livelihood, we want to make absolutely certain this will work completely."

Harding finally admitted what troubled him the most. Insurance guys typically come across as vultures but don't really have the backbone to get into a fight. Money is their incentive. These were basically two decent guys who liked to make as much of it as possible, without getting their hands soiled if at all possible.

I didn't argue about the fifteen-dollar daily rate despite my standard fee of twenty-five as a private investigator. I made that only when I was on a case; this would be regular work. They agreed to three percent for all recoveries but insisted on itemized receipts. Van Sickle provided me with a detailed description of the necklace.

My first stop was the Red Apple Filling Station on North Broadway. It was the regular hangout of Tyler Schenkel, a veteran like myself who chose the darker side of the street to walk. The counter was like his office. It was just as easy to find him there for breakfast, lunch, or dinner. The last time I saw him was when I handed him four twenties for basically acting as a decoy under the guise of a bodyguard. While he wasn't all smiles at my presence, he likely figured he might get some additional cabbage from me.

"I'm looking for a gold and diamond necklace," I stated simply.

"You see, this is what happens when you've got a

steady girlfriend," he replied.

"I hear Glen Hubbell, the property developer, has got a bad habit with the horses."

"That a fact?"

"Now, maybe he passes off a piece of jewelry to someone like you, figures you'll fence it somewhere quiet, take a cut, all while he's filing an insurance claim and getting full value for it. None of which, of course, will ever line your pockets."

The clink of the fork on his plate was the angriest sound I heard that morning. He wiped his lips with his napkin and turned to me sharply.

"I figured it sounded too good to be true."

"Sometimes legitimate businessmen are the biggest criminals, Tyler."

"Do I get something for my trouble?" His stare made it so it was not a pleading inquiry so much as a demand.

"Fifty." Going in, I calculated a recovery of seventy-five dollars. It was worth it to grease Tyler so I could make a good impression on my hopefully new employers. Tyler removed the trinket from his pocket and handed it to me slyly under the counter.

My next stop was the police station. I found Sergeant Richard Rogers from Robbery Division. Even though Eastborough had their own law enforcement division, I figured they might try to brush this under the rug. By ensuring the Wichita Police Department acted as a liaison, I could ensure transparency as well as documented verification of the recovery. I asked Rick to have a report made to that effect and get me a copy. I hung around for less than half an hour before I returned to Farmers and Bankers Life Insurance.

I explained to Troy Harding and Tom Van Sickle

that Glen Hubbell's gambling proclivities were well known and speculated the theft to be a fraud. After my own inquiries, the necklace was secured and handed over to the Wichita Police Department to be returned to Eastborough. I presented them with a copy of that report. Whereas I was unfamiliar with protocols with regard to such unusual circumstances, I strongly suggested the policy with Hubbell be terminated for cause as it was likely he may find himself incarcerated at some point in time.

The two of them stood there with their mouths agape.

It wasn't even lunch.

Chapter Sixteen

To be fair, it was really an easy audition. I knew about Hubbell's reputation as far back as my police days. At one point, Glick Helbert used him as a contractor on a project for Green Gables, a road house outside city limits on Thirteenth Street. It was purely guesswork that Tyler Schenkel would fence the goods. Otherwise, it might have taken me more of the afternoon to wrap the case up.

After he acknowledged my skills, Troy Harding sat me down to formally offer me the position. They didn't quite have a name for it as I was to be more than a researcher and not quite an adjuster. However, he established the foundation of the pay scale and then turned me over to Tom Van Sickle to get an overview of the myriad paperwork they were required to complete. In that regard, it was not unlike the police department. Overall, it would be as close to what I had previously done without getting shot at. There was no reason to argue with that.

For most of the rest of the week, I remained in my exceedingly small office. It contained a desk, a chair, a file cabinet, and a waste basket. There were no windows. None of this was worthy of complaints. Also, as I accepted the renumeration of the position with utter willingness, I could not issue forth grievances about income. I recalled from Ecclesiastes 5:10 – *He that loveth silver shall not be satisfied with silver; nor he that loveth abundance with increase: this is also vanity.* I tried to fit into the world as any other man would and find joy in simply walking this earth.

The members of Hebrew Congregation were, quite frankly, surprised to see me that Friday evening for Shabbos. Especially my father as I hadn't advised him of my attendance. We watched and listened as Rabbi Mendel led the services while the great Rabbi Saperstein sat proudly nearby, his eyesight nearly completely gone.

My thoughts were that if I took a step toward a more traditional job with the intentions of maintaining a life inspired by my parents, marriage, and family and all, I needed to take the first steps toward reestablishing a relationship with my temple. Eileen would have expected it as well.

Afterward, I spoke with members who exhibited their delight at my presence, several who made references to my service during the war, but no one once mentioned my occupation as a private detective. I didn't expect anyone to do so. I intended to move toward that elusive state called *normalcy*.

I wanted to share my progress with Eileen but not in any kind of celebratory manner. She accepted my invitation to dinner at the Pan American Café. Until King Mar, the owner and my dear friend, secured and made my own father's recipe for matzo ball soup, Eileen was not enamored of the place. She readily acquiesced, likely at the thought of latkes or rugelach.

When I uttered "I got a job," she almost dropped her spoon. I smiled in continued silence, which prompted her to goad me into some kind of elaborate recitation. I didn't listen to myself as I spoke, but it seemed I rambled on at a rather speedy pace. At times I cut myself off from one train of thought to leap into another. When I finished, Eileen very gently put her spoon down and looked at me with a grave concern.

"Are you doing this for me?" she asked softly.

"Well, in one regard, yes. For us, actually."

She reached across the table and held my hands in hers.

"Harold, I would love nothing more than to be your wife and start a family with you and honor the Lord Almighty and His laws. But, to do that, you have to be completely invested in that relationship. You need to devote your heart and soul into it. If you do this just for me, at what point in time will you regret your decision, regret me?"

At that moment, I was like the Israelites as they wandered in the desert. I had been unable to return to a profession in law enforcement. I could find no passion for the rabbinate. While I conceded the potential danger of a private investigator, I gave myself the opportunity to connect with people. In my zeal to fit in with a regular job, Eileen thought I turned away ever further from who I really was. The irony that struck me was I no longer could be certain of who that might be.

The conversation returned to a more amiable tone. I acknowledged her comments and feelings, suggested this could become substantial enough economically that might allow me more free time for Talmudic study, and asked her to be patient with this effort. Naturally, she showed how understanding she could be. I wondered, however, what she would have said had I proposed in the park prior to the Morgan-Smith case.

Over the next several weeks, I got used to the forms

and filing system, verified the death of a man insured by the firm was from a massive heart attack as he crossed the street, and confirmed the damage caused by a twister at the Arther Airport located in the 2800 block of West Pawnee. I chatted with Karla Duggan after the Carnegie Library finally got their microfilm reader they ordered back in 1940. The announcement of the opening of the 81 Drive-In seemed like a fun opportunity for Eileen and me.

Overall, I started to settle into a routine that began to give me a sense of comfort. I didn't feel the urge to analyze humanity or contemplate how the war changed us as a society. I still harbored the pangs of the loss of many friends and comrades but was at ease with how the Lord guided us all through difficult times. The cats took advantage of my newfound peace of mind, as well as my more regular hours, with their demands for frequent bouts of attention and additional food in their bowls. A stillness settled upon me.

It was on the evening of Sunday, September 15 that I heard a gentle knock at my door. It was almost apologetic in nature as though someone were reluctant to call my attention. Uncertain as to who it might be, I shuttered the cats behind the pocket doors and answered the inquiry.

Troy Harding stood alongside a gentleman who appeared to be in his late fifties. He was shorter than Troy but of a stout physique. Not overweight but well fed. His clothing was fashionable and stylish, but more the kind worn by successful businessmen than those with a more social agenda. They appeared rather rumpled as if he had been hit by a streetcar. His hair was thinning and his ears stuck out a bit. He slowly rubbed his hands together almost in anticipation of a harsh word. What struck me most was his look of despair mingled with ambivalence, as though he were worried but could not bring himself to be overly concerned about it, whatever it might be.

"Harold, I'm terribly sorry to bother you on a Sunday evening." My boss was gracious but continued to remain professional.

"No bother at all."

I opened the door wider and waved the two gentlemen through. They sat in the loveseat and I across from them in a chair. Something deeper than a silence hung like a cloud above us. A storm could well be expected and was soon to arrive.

"This is Mr. William Johnson. He's the Vice-President at People's Bank and Trust."

"Douglas and Main," I responded.

"Yes," Johnson popped up. "I'm largely in charge of commercial loans."

"How long have you been there?" My questions were designed to have him focus on easy topics to talk about, namely himself. We are more at ease when the subject is ourselves.

"Nearly twenty-eight years. Sixteen as Vice-President."

"Mr. Johnson has a life insurance policy with us," Harding interjected, then stopped cold. "Bill and I have been friends for a long time, Harold."

The brief introduction mixed business with personal but offered no indication of the importance of this visit. William Johnson leaned forward and spoke with a directness and clarity.

"This past Friday, the thirteenth, I vaguely recall

leaving work."

"I don't understand, Mr. Johnson."

"I spoke with my secretary, Mrs. Juliet Gallison, around three in the afternoon. She brought files of two recent loans that were approved. I would likely have reviewed and signed them and then left promptly at four o'clock."

"But you didn't?"

"I don't know."

I looked at Troy Harding. I hoped he didn't feel I had psychiatric abilities as well. I was about to issue forth my deep concerns about the conversation when William Johnson continued.

"I don't know what happened on Friday. Or Saturday. All I know is that I woke up this morning in a house wearing the same clothing I had on when I would have departed the bank. The same clothing you see me wearing now."

"Where was this house?"

"I can't be certain. I was rather, shall we say, groggy."

"Drunk?"

"No, sir," he said defiantly.

"Drugged?"

He had a quizzical look, one of speculation, as though he tried to describe in as clinical a fashion as possible what he experienced.

"Quite possibly."

Since he appeared to have no medical training, it was pointless to pursue that inquiry.

"What kind of house was it?"

"Two stories. Several rooms. Elegant wallpaper. Crystal chandeliers. Red velvet furniture. Oh my! I dare say it almost sounds like a brothel."

"Was it?"

He looked sharply at me, his character impugned by the suggestion. My instincts as an investigator caused these questions to come out as second-nature. I never worried that I would hurt a client's feelings if it elicited the truth.

"I don't know, Mr. Bergman. I just don't know. I did not encounter anyone there. As I said, my mind was in something of a fog. Things were blurry. I didn't see any scantily clad women or nervous gentlemen. I heard some muffled sounds. Perhaps. My goodness! I wouldn't be able to say for sure where I was even if I swore it on a stack of Bibles."

He slumped as his hands covered his face in embarrassment, even though he didn't know me until a few minutes prior. His own sense of propriety caused his shame. It was based more on speculation than recollection.

"You have to admit this is a troubling turn of events." I couldn't tell if Troy Harding spoke as a friend or someone who tried to protect an investment. "A man of Bill's prestige and importance in the community unable to determine where he had been for roughly thirty-six hours. There is something very nefarious about this."

It was a mystery to be certain, but I couldn't have agreed more with Harding.

"I'd recommend we contact the police at once." I sounded like my father or my rabbi.

"No." Johnson looked up suddenly, held his hands in front of him, and waved them as though he instructed a plane to not land. "It mustn't be done. I can't have that."

By his words, I recognized they both wanted to protect a personal interest, although for each it might have been different. For the last several weeks, I segued into the role of a glorified office worker in the insurance field. I longed to move forward but this conundrum pulled me back to solving dark riddles. I looked at Troy Harding inquisitively.

"I need you to help Mr. Johnson figure this out. You have the skills to do so. Probably even better than the police. And you can bring a degree of discretion into it that is sorely required. Naturally, we'll shift all of your other duties to Tom and the remaining adjusters. I'd like you to work on this full time." He ended with one word that transformed this from a job assignment to one of deeply humbling need. "Please."

"Mr. Johnson, what time do you get to the bank in the morning?"

"Precisely at eight."

"You'll advise Mrs. Gallison you made an appointment with me for eight thirty that you neglected to advise her of. Have her cancel all your other appointments for the remainder of the morning."

"I understand."

"Do you trust her?"

"She has been with me for fourteen years."

"Yes, sir, but do you trust her?"

He nodded affirmatively.

"I'm going to need to dig, Mr. Johnson. Think of me as Howard Carter in Egypt. I will ask direct questions. I will need honest and complete answers. Whatever they might be."

"Yes. I understand."

"Whatever you tell me will be in strictest confidence. Your answers will be used to determine the missing time from this past weekend. I can't guarantee any degree of success. But I need to know, right now, from both of you, if you will accept whatever it is I discover."

They both nodded as though they were tired children who stayed up too late. I suggested Mr. Johnson get home to bed and advised Troy Harding I would be in contact after I conducted my initial interview. I also asked him to refrain from sharing these events with anyone, including Tom Van Sickle, for the time. It was imperative to keep this investigation within the smallest circle possible.

When they left, I let the cats out. They seemed more bored than annoyed. For my part, I thought I would feel disappointed to take what I considered a step backward. Instead, I became charged and eager to step back into the darkness.

Chapter Seventeen

King's X was just around the corner from People's Bank and Trust. I figured it would be a good thing to start a very serious investigation with a full belly. Jennie Palmer watched me shovel eggs, toast, home fries, and down several cups of coffee. She figured something was afoot.

"You don't come in for weeks and then you eat as much as that guy from Los Angeles a while ago." She stood with the coffee pot while she waited for me to respond and spill the beans.

"Just as I stepped out of the game, I got pulled back in," I said with an air of mystery.

She poured my coffee and lightly nodded. The specifics were not significant; this teenage gal understood the world in a way wizened men couldn't.

I walked into the bank shortly after eight and to the desk where a young gentleman in proper business attire stood guard as a kind of receptionist. I mentioned I had an appointment with Mr. Johnson. He clicked on his intercom, spoke briefly, then looked up and smiled. I returned the smile. It would have been rude not to do so.

Within less than a minute, a stocky woman strutted directly toward me. It was like my time in the Ardennes as a tank strolled inexorably in my direction. She appeared no more than five foot five but had strong shoulders and the legs of a bull that were noticeable through her business attire. Marie Dressler was only slightly more attractive.

"Mr. Bergman?"

"Yes, ma'am."

"I am Juliet Gallison, Mr. Johnson's personal secretary. If you will follow me."

The way she spoke made me feel like I had no other choice. I could only wonder if she had somehow been a drill sergeant, She walked two steps ahead of me at a pace that would put a foot soldier to shame and spoke just as quickly.

"Mr. Johson advised me just this morning of an appointment he made with you on Friday," she continued. "Although I have no recollection of his mentioning it to me in the least."

"What did he say on Friday, Mrs. Gallison?"

"Something to the effect of a dinner engagement. But absolutely no mention of your appointment."

In her own way, she made me feel to blame for her inconvenience. She opened Johnson's office door, stepped aside while I entered, and then closed it behind her, swiftly yet quietly. One could see she was the peak of efficiency and deplored any deviation from it.

An ornate yet surprisingly comfortable wood chair sat across from William Johnson's large desk which was neat and organized. It contained all measure of files and ledgers as well as an exquisite brass pen set and green-globed lamp. I sat in a room filled with mahogany and leather, brass and crystal. It befitted of a man of importance in any field you could consider. The small leather notebook and stubby pencil I had paled in comparison.

"Mr. Johnson, I'd like to ask you a few questions,

kind of get to know you better."

"Certainly."

"How old are you, sir?"

"Fifty-seven."

"Married?"

"Widowed for the past seven years."

"Children?" He shook negatively. "Any other family members?"

"None. I was an only child as was my late wife."

"Do you maintain a relationship with any females?"

"Mr. Bergman," he said incredulously.

"Mr. Johnson, you were advised I would ask an array of questions. If this gap in your memory—"

"It is not an issue of memory, sir. It is lost time."

I placed my notebook and pencil on the desk, and then sat with my hands on my knees. I tried to appear as non-threatening as possible.

"This is an unfortunate situation, Mr. Johnson, one that might have a perfectly reasonable explanation or something indicative, as Mr. Harding stated, of a nefarious act. I mean to determine who you are as completely as possible in order to ascertain specifically what transpired. That means your character, your habits, and even your vices."

He started to speak in defense of the suggestion that he had any vices at all.

"None of us are perfect, Mr. Johnson. In spite of all appearances to the contrary."

He sunk in his chair, a deflated dirigible, and realized his desire for the truth required a walk through a gauntlet. In that regard, he became more like I had been.

"Since my wife's passing, I have resisted all social

engagements, even those that involved just other men."

"The Wichita Club, the Lions Club, the Scottish Rite Temple?"

"Yes, all of those. I have many acquaintances and business associates who have long offered me membership in those organizations. I have declined for a variety of reasons, conflict of interest being one."

"And yet, Mrs. Gallison alluded to a dinner engagement you spoke to her about on Friday."

"Unfortunately, I have no recollection of that."

"Who might you have accepted an offer from?"

I suspected his first impulse was to bark out "No one," then thought better of that. With his arms crossed and a finger that covered his lips in deep contemplation, he worked hard to reach back deeply into his life, beyond the mundane and routine, to seek just one notion that stood out different and apart from what he typically did.

"In the past two weeks, I have had encounters with two gentlemen who were new to the area. One was German, a professional of some sort. This would have been, oh, last Thursday the twelfth. He applied for a business loan which we declined."

"For financial reasons?" The tone in my voice made it clear I believed otherwise.

"Unfortunately, the war has left a bad taste in our mouth with regard to certain groups." At least he didn't hide his bigotry.

"Who was the other one?"

"A doctor. A British doctor."

"A physician?"

"I'm not certain. He introduced himself as Dr. It was Kingston or Kingsley or Kensington."

"Where was this?"

"I was at dinner with the bank president and another man the week before last. Mrs. Gallison would have my schedule."

I instructed Johnson to call Mrs. Gallison into the office after an indication I would identify myself more specifically. He made gestures toward hesitancy, but I assured him of my discretion. When she walked in, she looked directly at her employer. I spoke strongly and forced her attention in my direction.

"Mrs. Gallison, I have been retained to investigate a matter of utter importance to Mr. Johnson that requires your complete cooperation and judiciousness. Am I perfectly clear?"

Her mouth was agape as her head swiveled back and forth between us. Johnson's gentle nod was the reassurance she needed.

"Yes, sir."

"Mr. Johnson went to dinner with the bank president the week before last. Can you get me the name of the establishment, please?"

"It was the Ledart Restaurant on East Central on Tuesday the Third, right after Labor Day." Given my brief encounter with Mrs. Gallison, I should not have been surprised by her recollection or grasp of Johnson's schedule, whether it was past, present, or future. "It was a meeting with Hobart Brady, president of the Chamber of Commerce."

"Mrs. Gallison, does the name Kingston or Kingsley or Kensington ring a bell at all?"

"No, sir."

"Do you have any indication whatsoever of Mr. Johnson's dinner engagement of this past Friday?"

"None at all. Mr. Johnson's business-oriented

schedule is logged and documented. This might have been of a more personal nature." She stopped herself suddenly and then glanced over at Johnson out of embarrassment.

"That will be all, Mrs. Gallison."

With that she departed. I sat in my chair with a blank stare. A lot of information in a very short period of time does not equal a qualified resolution. There was, at the very least, a few threads to pluck.

I told Johnson I would need to get the loan application from the German man to determine who he might be. He would also need to reach out to the bank president and Hobart Brady to inform them of my pending inquiries. It would be easier, I suggested, to claim to look for the British gentleman he encountered. I could easily question the staff at the restaurant without a need to mention anyone else.

I tucked the notebook and pencil into my pocket and shook Johnson's hand warmly. I intended to evoke a measure of confidence this wasn't still just a wild goose chase despite my own concerns. As I reached for the door knob, William Johnson called to me.

"A funny thing occurred to me, Mr. Bergman."

"Oh?"

"A very strange expression crept into my sleep last night and hasn't left my mind since."

"What is it?"

"Vulgar tin mouse. Strange, isn't it?"

"It's likely a product of extreme stress. Try your best to get back into your normal routine. It will likely give you a sense of comfort."

A man has no recollection of his whereabouts or activities from Friday evening through Sunday morning and rolls an inscrutable expression repeatedly around his mind. I could not honestly imagine even the most rigorous routine that could create any sense of comfort.

Chapter Eighteen

As I started to leave, Mrs. Gallison approached me in a quickened pace. She held a piece of paper. When she handed it to me, I saw it to be the primary loan application. The residence given by Wilhelm Bradenhorst was the Hotel Lassen.

"Rather unusual, wouldn't you say?" I inquired.

"One of the many reasons his application was denied."

"I'll return this to you when I'm through."

"No need," she spoke quickly. She went from a majordomo to a deeply concerned co-worker. "It is disheartening to see Mr. Johnson in such distress. Whatever you can do to, well, mitigate it would be highly preferred."

She had no awareness of any of the specifics but felt, as both an utter professional as well as a caring soul, something was gravely wrong. She expressed that concern in cautioned words.

I nodded, my face blank with the intention of not meaning this to be an emotional departure. Her revelation as quite human impressed me.

The Hotel Lassen was just around the corner, across the street from the Pan American Café. For all the times I dined with King Mar, I never paid that much attention to the hotel. It had a charm to it, not unlike other buildings downtown. Now, I had to consider it held someone who might be considered shady or not.

The front desk clerk at this hour of the day was a refined young woman, perhaps ten years older than myself, attractive in a very mature fashion, with a stylish wardrobe and deeply red lips to match hazel eyes. Her smile, when she saw me approach, was gracious but not necessarily inviting. She maintained a steady professionalism.

"I believe you have a Wilhelm Bradenhorst staying here," I declared plainly.

She immediately went to a card file, perused it with just one index finger, and began to shake her head negatively.

"Mr. Bradenhorst checked out this past Friday. The thirteenth." She paused. "Not very lucky, wouldn't you say?" There was not any witticism associated with the comment.

"Did he leave any kind of forwarding address?"

"No, sir."

My frustration probably came across my face as perplexed.

"Is this an urgent matter?" she inquired.

Quicker than Augie Galen switching sides of the plate, I put my mind into gear.

"Well, I'm a loan officer with People's Bank and Trust. You know, right around the corner?"

"Oh, yes."

"He came in to apply for a loan last Thursday and, as you can imagine, it is a bit of a process and it seems Mr. Bradenhorst was just a tad frustrated. He kind of, well, to be perfectly honest, stormed out of the bank in a rather impolite manner. But as it turns out our underwriters approved it after all. And so expediently. It is awfully unfortunate that the wheels of business drag slowly. So, there is a wee bit of embarrassment here, if you can see what I mean."

I needed to catch my breath from this extemporaneous dissertation. It never occurred to me that acting skills would be required to be any kind of insurance investigator. I would need further lessons.

"Gee, I'm so sorry but I have no idea where he went."

"Did he mention where he was from originally or maybe any other acquaintances in town?"

"No. I'm afraid not." A serene silence stagnated, like that before a tornado. Then, she finally snapped to attention. "He did ask about restaurants in town. Asked me what I thought of the Ledart."

I tried desperately not to look impressed with her response, thanked her for her gracious assistance, and left, which allowed me to return to my normal personality.

My next stop was the Carnegie Library. Karla Duggan, my dear friend with vibrant red hair, a personality like Martha Raye, and a mind like Professor Einstein, had a knack for researching many newspapers from all over the country and finding information that even intelligence agencies would have difficulty locating. Hopefully, she could find one German.

I showed her the loan application. It contained a date of birth (October 13, 1897), local residence (Hotel Lassen), citizenship (United States), and occupation (architect), although a current employer was not listed. The reason for the loan was listed simply as "business."

"That's not much," Karla said. She didn't sound disappointed, merely challenged, which definitely appealed to her.

“The only thing I can confirm is he was at the Lassen until last Friday, checked in shortly before Labor Day. If he is a U.S, citizen, we might be able to track those records.”

“We?” she proclaimed inquisitively.

“Yes, well, you would be able to.”

She nodded.

I leaned in close to her. “I’ve got a bad feeling about this. I’m looking for a British doctor and a German architect. I’ve had enough of Europe for a while.”

It was almost a full two weeks after William Johnson went to a business dinner where he encountered the British doctor.

She patted me on the shoulder and then sent me on my way. She would attend to the research. I was left to handle my own emotions. I turned suddenly and blurted out William Johnson’s dream phrase. Karla stared at me blankly.

“Well, you have cats. That shouldn’t be a problem.”

“Vulgar tin mouse,” I repeated and enunciated each word. “Does that mean anything to you?”

“I’ll add it to my list.”

Before my next move, I had to strongly consider what I said to Karla about Europe. The war for me was about fighting one enemy: the Axis. It was easy to lump several groups together and to focus our collective energies against defeating them. The French were resilient but were overwhelmed by the Germans in 1940. The Brits withstood the Blitz but ran out of supplies. Spain, smartly, stayed out of the picture. While Pearl Harbor was a direct attack on us, it seemed at the time our aggression should have been directed toward the

Japanese. Nevertheless, the world was in disarray and order needed to be restored. It seemed to be the same story throughout history.

Once that happened, I desired simply to remain involved in the business of my community, my family, and my temple. This assignment, if you will, proved two vital things. The responsibilities of my job veered closer to my occupation as a private detective and blurred the distinction. Also, I came to understand the world was still in disarray.

My timing was off. It was just about the lunch hour at the Ledart. I grabbed a small table and ordered a chicken salad sandwich and a cup of tea. When I placed the order, I asked the waitress if she had worked the Tuesday after Labor Day or knew anyone there who did. She hadn't herself but promised to ask around.

I was there the better part of an hour. I casually finished my sandwich and sipped my tea. By the time it appeared I was finished, the waitress returned and found two one-dollar bills on the table.

"One is for you if you find someone who worked the Tuesday night after Labor Day. The other dollar is for them." I was polite. I smiled. I recognized the initial inquiry was not urgent enough when the possibility of lunchtime tips awaited. This offer beat that by a mile.

The waitress brought over a co-worker, a charming but young and inexperienced gal, probably about Jennie Palmer's age but without the savvy. My waitress grabbed her dollar and took off. The youngster stood awkwardly, almost confused.

"What's your name?" I asked softly.

"Patricia."

"So, you worked the dinner crowd the Tuesday after

Labor Day, Patricia?"

"Yes, sir."

"Do you remember seeing or hearing a British gentleman at all?"

She was in deep thought for a bit, but I couldn't tell if it was from her attempt to remember or lack of understanding the question.

"They talk funny, right?"

"Yeah, kind of like Cary Grant. Have you ever seen *Arsenic and Old Lace*?"

"Oh, yeah. That was funny." She stopped after the sentence and returned to a look of deep thought. "This guy didn't look nearly as good," she suddenly reported.

"So, there was a British gentleman here?"

"I remember now. He was talking to these three other men, fancy businessmen types, you know. They had a table, and this fella was standing talking with them. Was smack dab in the middle of the aisle and the waitresses had a hard time getting around him."

"If he didn't look like Cary Grant, what did he look like?"

"Big guy. Wouldn't call him fat or anything. Just, well, big. But really well-dressed. The kind of clothes you don't see that often."

"Because they're fancier than most?" I pressed.

"No. More like they were old. You know, the kind of stuff from probably before the war or further back even."

"Can you describe him?" While the sandwich was okay, this conversation got me salivating.

"Light brown hair but short and trimmed around the ears. One of those funny moustaches."

"Like a Mexican bandit?" I tried to be lighthearted

to avoid this sounding like an interrogation. She went into that contemplative pose again.

"Have you ever seen a movie called *Since You Went Away*?"

"Yeah."

"There was a British guy in that. He had a beard though and this guy, in the restaurant I mean, he just had that moustache."

She referred to Monty Woolley. I now had confirmation of this encounter. Naturally, it wasn't worthwhile to determine if she overheard any bits of the conversation. I might be able to reach out to the bank president or Hobart Brady at the Chamber of Commerce under some pretext.

I glanced at the dollar bill as acknowledgement of my offer. Patricia grabbed it and ran off.

As I got in my car, I realized that all I knew for sure was the existence of two men William Johnson had encountered over the last couple of weeks, who were new to him. One made a direct inquiry at the bank. The other might have been a casual conversation between men of a certain ilk.

I was tempted to visit Bradley Wolrebinski, the man who wrote lurid crime fiction, to get a take on this. To do so would be an admission I had run out of options. This was the first day and there was some progress. I figured I would call on Mr. Brady and tried to think of an adequate story on my drive over.

The receptionist at the Chamber of Commerce was dark haired with a shade of deep purple lipstick that gave her a moody and alluring appearance. Her dress was a black-and-white print that just as easily could have been hung in the Wichita Art Museum. For my performance,

I played the part of a put-upon junior executive.

"I am terribly sorry to bother you, but I'd like to see Mr. Brady, if he's available."

"He's a very busy man, Mr.—?"

"Bergman. I'm a new account executive at People's Bank and Trust. It seems Mr. Brady and my boss, Mr. Johnson, had dinner with the bank president a couple of weeks ago, and there was an item of, well, shall we say, discretion that needed to be asked."

"I'm certain Mr. Johnson can telephone Mr. Brady directly." She was well trained in her duties.

"This is a matter of discretion." I pronounced the last word in almost a hushed whisper, as though it were a military secret. It all seemed rather foolish. But since she picked up her phone and dialed a number, spoke softly, and then hung up, I imagine I was successful.

Hobart Brady was a fit looking man, dark hair that was graying on the sides. He stood immediately and walked over briskly to shake my hand before he directed me to the chair in front of his desk.

"So, you're one of Bill's new boys, huh?"

"Yes, sir."

"What can I do for you that is a matter of discretion?" His pronouncement of the word was more lighthearted.

"Well, Mr. Johnson indicated there was a gentleman who interrupted your dinner at Ledart right after Labor Day and thought he might be a viable business prospect. The problem is Mr. Johnson lost track of the man's name and where he could be reached."

"Oh, yes, I remember him. Pompous sort. Then again, the Brits are known as such. His name was Kingsley. Dr. Douglas Kingsley. Not exactly sure what he was a doctor of now that I think of it. It's rather surprising that Bill would think of him as a business prospect."

"Oh?"

"This Dr. Kingsley was a member of some fraternal organization. Claimed the three of us would be suitable members. Chuck Michaelson, the bank president, and I aren't into that kind of social gathering. However, ever since Bill's wife passed, he has looked for something to, you know, break out of his shell."

That comment surprised me. Johnson indicated he preferred his solitude.

"This is awfully embarrassing, Mr. Brady."

"Don't think anything of it. If this winds up being good for Bill, it would certainly be worthwhile."

I thanked him for his time and left. I had a name and a reason for an interaction. Where Bradenhorst fit in was still to be determined. I rushed to the Carnegie Library and got hold of a Polk directory. Kingsley, Douglas, Dr. 1149 West Thirteenth Street North. Riverside. I shuddered when I finally realized Karla Duggan hovered over my shoulder.

"You want me to look him up, too?"

"Certainly easier given the fact he lives in town, wouldn't you think?"

"I've got the scoop on your German guy."

I should not have had such a surprised look on my face. In a neatly written script, the paper she handed me identified Wilhelm Bradenhorst, born on October 13, 1897, who attended the "Königliche Baugewerkschule", or Royal School of Building Trades, in 1914, but was soon drafted into the army. He completed his education after the war and received a degree in architecture and civil engineering. At that point, she had not secured any citizenship records.

It had been a busy morning for both of us.

Chapter Nineteen

The color of my car, the aptly named Sir Pounce-mobile by my impish librarian friend, was not conducive to surveillance or use on a stakeout. To drive randomly around Riverside would leave an impression on anyone who might perchance take notice. I assumed most people would. I made one solo pass along Thirteenth Street. The large brick homes, mostly in a Tudor styling, were separated from the street either by iron fences or brick walls. Such was the case with house number 1149. I turned north onto Garland Street and parked a little more than half a block up the road.

It was a pleasant enough day, but a strong wind blew. It almost knocked me off my feet. My ankle held up well enough for a minor jaunt even with the breeze. I certainly didn't think I would need to climb any walls. At least I hoped not.

From across the street, the house appeared relatively tall. The mature adult trees blocked the view of second-story windows. It wasn't as sprawling as the house next to it. However, the walls extended on both sides of the property. There would have been no use in driving clear across to Oak Park as the trees there would have blocked my view of Kingsley's back yard. From all sides, a complete view of the house was inaccessible.

My next thought was to visit the Registrar of Deeds and seek the public records on the property. I squashed that idea almost immediately. All I would be able to determine was the name of the owner, which I already knew. Additionally, an inquiry of that sort could trigger awareness by those one might wish to elude. I needed to remain anonymous for as long as possible.

I sat in my car and mentally reviewed the characters I discovered. One was a German who tried to open a business account. The other, an Englishman who supposedly attempted to engage a quiet man into the world of fraternal orders. I saw no direct connection between the two nor could determine how either would result in William Johnson with no memories of an entire day and a half of his life. Perhaps these characters were not involved with the incident. Then again, with Johnson a solitary individual, any encounter might be valid.

After my interview with him that morning, I eliminated the possibility the Vice-President of People's Bank and Trust went for a bit of debauchery and concocted a bizarre story to hide his indiscretions. Troy Harding would not have allowed it to besmirch Farmers and Bankers Life Insurance. No, something happened to William Johnson and not because of anything he did. I was less then twenty-four hours into this inquiry and already stumped.

A few quiet moments in the synagogue would help clear my mind and put me on a better path toward understanding the complexity of this unique situation. Rabbi Mendel greeted me at the door as I entered. Despite his slender appearance and gaunt face, he was a man of amazing strength, the kind it takes to fight evil and come out ahead. I knew little of his life, but he impressed me nevertheless.

"Will you be attending Rosh Hashanah services with

us this year, Harold?"

"When is it, *rebbe*?"

"A week from Thursday."

"It is my intention to be here with my father."

"And will Miss Horowitz and her parents be joining us as well?"

I couldn't tell if he saw what passed for a smile on my face.

"I will certainly ask."

We walked slowly, side by side. Throughout my life, it seemed to me that clergymen of all denominations walked slowly, never in any rush to get from one point to another. The simplicity of movement preserves one's vision, as it is stated in Ta'anit 10b – *Do not take long strides, as the Master said: A long stride takes away one five-hundredth of a person's eyesight, and this loss is not worth the time saved.*

"Is there any evil greater than that which you have witnessed, Rabbi Mendel?" My question was sudden, even to me.

"There is always a greater evil, Harold."

"Oh? And what is that?"

"The one we have yet to see. The one hiding in the shadows waiting for our greatest moment of weakness."

I understood that exceptionally well when I considered the fields and forests of war, the enemy who waited for you to tire or take a wrong step. We pushed ourselves beyond all measure to stay alive. Yet all of us knew, felt in our hearts, the war would end. What Rabbi Mendel described was a presence to be perpetually on guard to fight against.

"Some would call that Satan, *rebbe*."

"And some, Harold, would call it *yetzer hara,* the

evil inclination of man."

"What do we arm ourselves with when we do not know this evil nor can see it?"

"Be strong and of a good courage, fear not, nor be afraid of them; for the Lord thy God, he it is that doth go with thee; he will not fail thee nor forsake thee."

Those evil desires were in us all. Yet the strength I required was already within me. I just needed to remind myself of it occasionally.

The late afternoon and a weariness approached about the same time. My resolve still held strong but the mental energy I expended thus far drove me to feel tired beyond measure. My final visit of the day to the library rejuvenated me, especially when Karla seemed giddy with excitement.

"This guy is the real McCoy," she proclaimed without further explanation.

"I assume you can tell me something considerably more than that."

"Douglas Price Kingsley. Born September 18, 1880."

"Splendid. We can celebrate his birthday on Wednesday."

"Graduated with honors from Trinity College at the age of eighteen and then studied anatomy under Viscount Addison at Sheffield School of Medicine. I mean, the guy was a full-fledged surgeon by the time he was twenty."

"Keep going."

"So, World War I breaks out and they offer this guy a sweet position coordinating field hospitals but from all the way back in London. He declines and wants to work right in the field hospitals. You know, like on the front lines. They've got no choice but to send him. And, boy, his record is filled with commendations and medals. The British War Medal. The Victory Medal. The Territorial Force War Medal. The 1914-1915 Star. Eight field commendations. Three field promotions. It's amazing this guy can walk with all the metal they pinned to his chest."

"Okay, the man is an English hero."

She seemed dismayed I took Dr. Kingsley's war record so lightly in her estimation.

"Second Battle of the Marne during an Allied counter-offensive, he suffered a concussion from a shell that exploded behind him. He was in a hospital for two weeks before they shipped him home late summer of 1918. Apparently, it took a long time to recover and some questions arose about him continuing as a surgeon."

"Any reference anywhere you can find to fraternal organizations or secret societies?"

"Was associated with the Odd Fellows in college but nothing after the war."

"Did you find anything about that 'vulgar tin mouse'?"

"No. Are you sure that's what he said?"

"Yeah, but I'm not sure that's what he heard."

Karla got all my thanks and a promise for proper recompense. I left even more perplexed. A British doctor who was ostensibly a war hero had every right to be a member of a fraternal organization. Odd Fellows were largely based on revelry and camaraderie, but there were those who crossed over into Freemasonry, which from time to time throughout history encountered negative connotations.

I still could not fathom how any of that would lead to the lapse in Johnson's memory. I needed to gain more information about the comings and goings of Dr. Kingsley, and I needed to be more discreet than my vehicle would allow.

Richie Mayer, my young friend who drove a hack for the longest time, moved nearly three months prior to Colorado on account of his asthma. Another driver, Charlie Argento, married with three young daughters, was always on the lookout to earn some extra cabbage even if it meant a step or two outside of his legal comfort zone.

A double sawbuck allowed me to rent him and his cab for the evening. We parked in the same area on Garland Street. Just after sundown, close to eight o'clock, a big shiny black car came slowly out from the front gate. Charlie whistled as though he were at a burlesque show.

"Cadillac V-16 Phaeton. 1939 would be my guess." He spoke as though he recited the haftara at his bar mitzvah.

"How much does a car like that cost?" I asked naively.

"Five grand easy. And with whatever extras he added, you can probably say seven." He whistled again. A hack driver with three daughters would never own one of those.

I instructed Charlie to be as careful as possible following the car. I did not want to put us in an awkward or dangerous position. Kingsley made one stop in College Hill. He entered a home and emerged within less than five minutes. I took down the address in my notebook. The other stop was more surprising. It was on

East Ninth Street, not too far from the De Luxe Barber Shop which was in a colored section of town. The building had a closed business on the main floor but stairs that led to a second story. Kingsley traversed the steps in less time than the house in College Hill. Perhaps a knock on a door and then a quick departure?

He stopped at the Broadview Hotel. As Charlie drove past a couple of times, we saw the good doctor enjoy libations at the lobby bar. No one sat with him that we noticed. He stayed for nearly half an hour before he left and went home.

"What's this all about, Mr. Bergman?" While Charlie was grateful for the extra cash, the innocuous driving around time had him confused to the point of caution. I felt the same way.

Chapter Twenty

The gentle knock on my door the next morning was not the surprise. The owner of the hand knocking was. It was Dr. Douglas Price Kingsley, dressed as though it were evening and he had reservations for one of the finer dining establishments in town. For all I knew, that could be his standard wardrobe. I failed to ask Karla about the attire of English heroes. I was already dressed myself, had drunk my coffee and ate my toast, but not before I fed the cats. Their bowls were on the kitchen floor. Astonishingly, they remained under the kitchen table. They were typically gregarious and curious. This time they were reserved.

"Yes?" I reminded myself quickly that I wasn't actually supposed to know him. Fortunately, my brain worked well that morning.

"You are Harold Bergman, correct?"

"Yes, I am."

"I'm Douglas Kingsley. Dr. Douglas Kingsley. Might I enter?"

With one hand, I pulled the door open wider. I waved him toward me to indicate entry was acceptable. Once I closed the door, I pulled the pocket doors shut.

"I have no allergy or aversion to felines," he declared.

"It's not you I'm worried about, doctor. Have a seat, please."

He took the settee and covered a large part of it with his girth. He reminded me of a fancier version of Max Burke, the Los Angeles mug who helped me locate Debra Rose Nathan and break up a spy ring.

"I'd like to inquire about availing myself of your services."

"I beg your pardon?"

"I'm looking for a gentleman who owes me a considerable sum of money. He appears to be avoiding me and now I can't locate him."

For a moment, I was perplexed. Then it occurred to me I had left the sign outside the apartment that identified me as a private investigator even though I was now under the employ of Farmers and Bankers Life Insurance. I also had to wonder whether his presence here was coincidental or planned in some fashion.

"My apologies, Dr. Kingsley, but I am no longer in private practice."

Though the words flowed out of my mouth naturally, I got a sharp pain in my side when I realized I tried to throw away an opportunity to learn more about him given his somewhat ephemeral connection to William Johnson.

"Quite a pity." His accent was not boldly English. It had almost a washed-out sound to it, as though he traveled in America for enough time to have some of the pomposity melt away. He more than made up for it by his demeanor.

"Perhaps I could direct you toward a viable resolution?" I hoped my professionalism did not come across as overly eager.

"A few years before the war, I was introduced through certain professional connections to a gentleman who was soliciting to establish a business in the heart of London. His proposal seemed well-founded, and I made him a loan with an acceptable return within eighteen months. Naturally, the war began, the business venture never went through, and this man was unwilling to return any portion of the investment."

"How much?"

"One thousand pounds."

I don't usually whistle. Such an amount brought it out of me automatically.

"Was he pressed into service?"

"Perhaps so. He was German. I wasn't mindful of his presence in England for the duration of the war nor had I the means to determine his whereabouts."

"He might have been killed."

He shook his head.

"After the war I was made aware he had come to the States with the same portfolio, again seeking funds."

"And how did this information come to you?"

He waved his hand as though brushing away flies.

"I have many acquaintances in many fields, Mr. Bergman. Throughout Europe, the United States, and all over the world actually."

"Perhaps one of those acquaintances could be more useful in this endeavor."

He raised an eyebrow, cocked his head, and was convinced of my disinterest. At that moment, I could not consider him any kind of a threat to Mr. Johnson simply from this exchange. The early reference I received about his membership in a fraternal order did not come out in conversation.

"I'm sorry to have taken up your time, Mr. Bergman."

"I do have contacts within the police department having formerly been an officer myself. Perhaps I could provide this man's name to them and if they wind up hearing anything I could certainly pass that information along to you."

"Would you? That is a very gracious offer."

"What is the man's name?"

"Bradenhorst. William Bradenhorst. Although I suppose it might be Wilhelm for all I know."

It was as though Joe Louis hit me in the gut and knocked every last ounce of wind out of me. The man who tried to open an account at People's Bank and Trust seemed to be some kind of European con man. By the same token, this English doctor had coincidentally crossed paths with William Johnson. This became more muddled than mere coincidence would allow.

"If you do determine anything, I can be reached at Amherst 7-3473. And certainly, Mr. Bergman, you will be well compensated."

He left briskly and assuredly. I was now part of a Rube Goldberg machine. I searched my memory for all my readings and could not recall any word in Hebrew for 'coincidence.' Jews believe everything is the will of God, foreseen and planned by He alone. Yet my simple unadorned mind wandered like a child as I tried to discern who of the two was the villain in this scenario. More than that, why did whatever happened to William Johnson take place? What was the purpose? To a Jew, our purpose is to seek a future that will be in some small measure better than the present. Unfortunately, as far as I could tell, neither Dr. Kingsley nor Mr. Bradenhorst were Jewish.

To locate records in Europe from before the war

would be difficult. With so many communities damaged or destroyed it was unlikely I would be able to locate substantive documentation on Bradenhorst in London much less anywhere in Germany. All I could focus on was what I knew for certain and what I could investigate here in Wichita.

I went to the Carnegie Library, grabbed the Polk Directory, and sat off in a dark unobtrusive corner. The house in College Hill listed a Christophe Blanc as owner. This European connection continued. I assumed this Blanc to be French. The building on East Ninth was identified as the Single Truth Church. I found a listing up until 1943 after which nothing else seemed to occupy the building. I knew someone who could guide me.

When Alonzo Washington got inadvertently caught up with a crooked cop all to earn a few extra dollars, his wife Althea had the presence of mind to reach out to me. I found him and got him cleared of any legal difficulties, not to mention saving his life. The police preferred roasting one of their own bad fish. Since that time, I was a welcome member of their home. Right on the front porch, a charming colored woman hugged a Jewish white man. And no one dared say a word.

"Alonzo's at work right now, Mr. Bergman."

"Still at Cudahy?"

"Yes, sir."

"Good for him. Well, you know, maybe you can help me. You ever hear of the Single Truth Church?"

"Weren't no church I'd ever go to," she said with a bit of a shudder.

"Oh?"

"Some sharp called himself Roberto Foster set up the place. Said he found the Single Truth and a path to the Lord. Started during the war. Didn't last but a year. Surprised it made it that far."

"What happened to Foster?" She shrugged her shoulders. "What's with the building now?"

"Squatters mostly. Mr. Theo Sayers, he owns the De Luxe Barber Shop, got his hands full keeping the riffraff out of his place."

We chatted a bit more. She told me about their plans for Christmas this year and invited me even though she knew I didn't celebrate. To her, I gave their household back its life and for that she would be forever grateful.

My father didn't accept the notion of me just dropping by late in the afternoon. We would either make plans to have dinner together or go to temple. Casual and sudden appearances were a dead giveaway that something was wrong. Perhaps my turn as a detective was based on inherited traits.

"Come in. I'll make some tea."

This act of boiling water and getting out cups and saucers was similar to cleaning the house before Passover to remove the *chametz,* the unclean food. The ritual of the tea was to clean the mind of thoughts that would weigh us down.

We sipped our tea and never looked at each other. When the time was right, my father knew, I would speak.

"It is one thing to be confused but still another for someone to intentionally confuse you." It was a stark, almost empty thing to say, a comment unrelated to anything else. Yet my father was a man who could see inside me by latching onto my words.

"*In quietness and confidence shall be your strength.*" At times, all we needed was to hear what we already knew. "Your greatest asset, Harold, has always been to think out a problem in quiet contemplation. Allowing someone to confuse you?" He shook his head almost in disappointment, but more to encourage me. "A man who is taller or broader or who has the physique of Samson could defeat you. But your mind is as great as Solomon's."

We continued to sip our tea in silence for a bit, then pushed the empty cups forward and sat, heads bowed in prayer. We spoke our own words in our minds directly to the Lord. I could only guess my father beseeched Adonai to guide me. I gave my thanks to the Lord for my father.

I stopped by the Pan American for an early dinner. The open-faced roast beef sandwich was covered in brown gravy for which several napkins were required. I started to write the name 'Kingsley' on one napkin, then 'Bradenhorst' on another. I took two more napkins. I wrote 'Blanc' on one, and 'Church' on the other. They sat on the table to my left. I moved them around like they were chess pieces.

Two men had a connection to each other. These two men crossed paths, even remotely, with William Johnson. If Bradenhorst was a con artist who tried to secure a loan from the bank, I couldn't imagine him kidnapping Johnson. He might have drugged him and had photos taken of Johnson in a compromising position. Without a wife, the possibility of blackmail might only have jeopardized Johnson's standing at the bank. Not much leverage there.

Kingsley, the medical prodigy and apparent war hero, supposedly had designs on Johnson as a member of an unknown fraternal organization. Mostly harmless, although history offered examples of such groups that were considerably more deadly and nefarious. Nothing specifically had presented itself during our brief meeting.

I pushed those two napkins away and brought the other two closer. I would need to research the Frenchman in order to determine his background. The former church might make a hiding place for someone else involved in a potential scheme. Then again, I couldn't imagine someone of any bearing and breeding, the kind that would be necessary to enter into Johnson's circle, living even temporarily in the shack that building became. I then pulled Kingsley's napkin toward the one that said 'Church.' Kingsley himself had stopped by that place, went up the stairs, and then came right down.

Why?

The dinner crowd started to pick up. I crumpled the napkins and set them on the plate with the remaining brown gravy. I made sure to smile at King Mar on my way out. I did not want him overly concerned either. At times, he could be as worried as my own father.

The cats were given their nightly repast. I sat in my favorite chair, turned on the radio, and caught an old timey country music show on KLH. I didn't think the cats were favorable toward that kind of music. Nevertheless, they jumped up and sat on either side of me, not necessarily requiring any attention. It was as though they sensed my need for stillness in the middle of a storm.

The only clear cut and logical conclusion I was able to come up with was a scheme so foreign to my thoughts or experience that I had yet to stumble upon it. And then I recalled the admonition of Rabbi Mendel regarding the greater evil:

The one we have yet to see. The one hiding in the

shadows waiting for our greatest moment of weakness.

I would need to be vigilant and strong.

Chapter Twenty-One

There are many words you could use to describe a white man who entered a barber shop in a predominantly colored neighborhood. Unless, of course, I was that white man. The work I did for Alonzo and Althea Washington as well as my brief association with wealthy businessman Josiah Howard gave me 'friend of the family' status, so to speak. Perhaps being a minority in that I was Jewish gave me a level of equality but just as likely the attitude was more of tolerance than outright acceptance. In either case, no heads turned too dramatically when I walked into the De Luxe Barber Shop in the twelve-hundred block of East Ninth Street.

Sullivan Starks was the primary barber when the owner, Theo Sayers, wasn't in. Sullivan was of medium height and build, although I figured he had a boxing background. He was a solid man who looked as though there were a trigger to be pulled just below the surface. His hair was closely cropped, and he sported a pencil-thin moustache that clung precariously to his upper lip. He was always cordial but not openly friendly. At least not to me.

"Howdy, Mr. Bergman."

His genial tone indicated he no longer held a grudge due to a divorce case I handled involving his cousin.

"Hey, Sully."

"You looking for Mr. Sayers?"

“No. Just a trim if it’s all the same.”

Sullivan looked over my shoulder toward the older gentleman who sat in one of the other chairs who acted as though he read yesterday’s paper.

“Ain’t they got barbers in your part of town?”

“Oh, well, I just happened to be in the neighborhood, figured I’d not waste the opportunity.”

He made his point but wasn’t about to turn away business. I didn’t have many sartorial skills and few opportunities to present myself in social settings. Yet I knew it was important to present an appearance of cleanliness and modesty.

Sullivan Starks clipped hairs from the back, combed my coiffure into a style fitting for my age and race, and dusted my neck with talcum powder. Within ten minutes he was done to his satisfaction, mine notwithstanding.

“What do I owe you?” I asked demurely.

“Twenty-five cents.”

“Prices have gone up.”

“Talk to Mr. Sayers.”

I placed two quarters in his hand which he kept open. He looked at the coins and then slowly at me. His eyes were a mix of uncertainty and pleasure.

“I’m guessing this ain’t for the next time,” he said softly.

“Roberto Foster. The Single Truth Church.”

“Man weren’t even colored,” he answered contemptuously. “Creole from somewhere in Louisiana. Got a whole bunch of ladies riled up. He was run out by some of our more conscientious citizens. Mostly husbands. Took them long enough if you ask me.”

“And the building?”

“Rat trap as far as I can tell.”

"Suppose there are squatters on that second story?"

"Could be," he replied, nodding as though the idea made sense.

"Thanks."

I started to leave.

"Mr. Bergman." His voice sounded almost confused. I turned while at the door. "You could have just asked."

"I know."

A pleased smile crossed his lips.

I had no idea who owned the building that formerly held the Single Truth Church. To enter it without the permission of the owners could be considered trespassing or breaking and entering which I knew from my days in the police department. I figured I would be able to come up with an explanation that might fall under 'reasonable suspicion' if anyone from law enforcement were to ask.

I shielded my eyes and looked through the front window, but the sun behind me created a bit of glare. The inside was empty with the exception of one podium likely used as an altar of some sort, many blank papers strewn around the floor, and quite a bit of dust. Consequently, I could determine there were no footprints and hence no one traipsing around this lower level recently. That left me with the second floor.

As a police officer, I might have my gun drawn and gone up the steps in a manner befitting my training at the academy. Since I no longer carried a gun, I used my military experience, my instincts, and my faith.

I took two steps, stopped, and listened, then proceeded in the same fashion. I didn't hear a thing. One lone door was at the top of the stairs. I had to choose between a brash entrance, a knock, or a quiet entry. I chose the latter. With a handkerchief, I turned the knob slowly until it finally clicked. I opened the door barely an inch, waited to determine if I noticed any sound, then proceeded to push it open completely but still cautiously. The first thing I noticed was a small empty desk and a chair. Beyond the chair, a small washroom with a toilet and sink. Across from the door, another room with its door closed but not fully shut.

Each step I took involved placing my foot down as quietly as possible. I moved as though I had no other place to be. I hugged the wall next to the far door and pushed on it slowly with one hand. I saw a man's foot on a cot. I stopped and waited. No sound and no movement. I threw the door open all the way.

One arm dangled off the bed. One leg was straight while the other was bent under the body. When I moved closer, I saw a face contorted in extreme agony, dried spittle on the corners of the mouth, eyes fixed on the ceiling as though in utter shock and surprise. The man was most certainly dead.

I went to the De Luxe and stuck my head just inside the door.

"Sully, call the police and send them to that dilapidated church."

"Squatters?"

"Not quite."

Detective Melvin Baumgartner was surprised to see me not only at a crime scene but in this part of town. When a passport inside the dead man's jacket pocket confirmed him to be Wilhelm Bradenhorst, I indicated this was a man I looked for as it pertained to bank business and nothing criminal per se. Certainly none that

I knew for certain. At that point, I still came across as a private detective and not an insurance company employee working on an unrelated matter.

"All right, I'll keep you up to date on this," Mel offered, "but you've got to tell me everything you know. Don't make this difficult for me, Harold."

I took the opportunity to talk with Dr. Gerhardt, the chief medical examiner, as he left. He must have been close to seventy with thick coke-bottle glasses, thinning white hair, and enough crags and lines in his face to depict a lifetime of experience.

"What does it look like to you?"

"No bullet or stab wounds. My guess is some kind of poison."

"Couldn't it have been a heart attack?"

"At first appearance, yes. But there is a brownish color on the fingertips, bloating of the belly, and a stench of garlic or onions that is not consistent with a heart attack."

"Can you tell what kind of poison?"

His head shake was an indication he told me all he knew for the moment based on a cursory examination. Detective Baumgartner pulled me away as though it were time for bed, and I insisted on staying up late.

I sat at his desk in utter boredom while he made a series of phone calls, talked with other policeman who passed, some of whom acknowledged my presence, and basically did his best to keep me out of the sort of trouble he expected me to get into. Nearly an hour later, he finally addressed me.

"Wilhelm Bradenhorst. Born 13 October 1897." He proceeded to outline his place of birth and education, all of which I had learned from Karla Duggan but didn't admit to for fear of insulting him. He finally got to the parts I needed to be filled in. Bradenhorst was a conscientious objector in late 1939 and was held in prison until 1945 when the Allies released him and other political prisoners. There is no further mention until he entered the country back on April 9 of this year on a six-month work visa. The signatory on the work application was Dewey Purcell, Vice President of Loans at Commonwealth Bank of Boston. However, Bradenhorst's whereabouts were unknown until his loan application at the bank in Wichita, a piece of information I was obligated to divulge, and then his subsequent death. Mel Baumgartner tried to get hold of this Dewey Purcell only to learn he died of a massive heart attack back on May 8.

I wasn't sure if there was a lump in my throat or if I started to get nauseous. Bradenhorst was connected, at least circumstantially, with Dr. Kingsley and more directly with Dewey Purcell. How this Christophe Blanc fit in remained a mystery. I knew the importance of this to both William Johnson and Troy Harding. I based my entire brief career as a private investigator on the tenets of honesty, integrity, and discretion. This, however, felt a lot like being on the Titanic. I knew I most definitively needed a life jacket.

I told Mel what I knew but not why I was involved. Johnson was adamant about not bringing the police into this investigation, but I was in over my head. My brief explanation was the suspicious nature of Bradenhorst's application and the encounter by bank executives with Kingsley. I had to admit my discovery of Blanc through surveillance. Mel actually thought I did admirable police work and made a half-hearted reference toward my return to the department. I was grateful for my friends.

"If the medical examiner's office finds a determination of death by poison, we would have reasonable cause to interview this Dr. Kingsley."

"Yes, but," I responded, "this guy is far too clever for you to haul him in to try to sweat him out. There's really nothing behind it all. Right?"

"He was looking for Bradenhorst, wasn't he? And then he found him. Or so you say. Now this guy is dead."

"He was up and down those stairs in no time. For all I know, Bradenhorst wasn't there and Kingsley never spoke with him. There is no corroborative eyewitness."

Mel sat silently and suddenly realized this case offered no evidence of any actual crime at this point. If Kingsley wanted to find Bradenhorst for the express purpose of getting his money back, there would have been no value in killing him. You can't squeeze blood from a stone.

"We could put this death under wraps for a day or so, you could reach out to Kingsley, and offer to help him."

"Or I could tell him I found Bradenhorst and offer to solve his death and try to recoup the funds." I fell into the middle of an English drawing room mystery; it was a game with murder. Only a feeling deep within me sensed I would wind up coming face to face with a greater evil.

Melvin Baumgartner, detective in the Wichita Police Department and fellow Jew, leaned in close to me.

"This isn't the kind of thing you play around with."

"I know."

"No, listen to me, Harold. From everything I can tell, Wilhelm Bradenhorst came into this country under false pretenses, lied to a banker in Boston, and finally made it here to Kansas where he tried to con another bank out of money. There's no next of kin. I think if I talk with Dr. Gerhardt, we can forego the autopsy and call it death by natural causes. Don't you think it would be better that way?"

I understood what Mel was doing, not only for the department, but mostly for me. While I couldn't be specific on the reasons, I made it clear to him this needed attention. How much bigger I just couldn't be certain.

"You get a drip from the ceiling, you put a bucket under it. It collects too much water, it floods your house. You wear boots until you need a boat. And then the dam finally bursts and everyone drowns. It would be a lot easier to patch the roof than to let it get that far."

He nodded at me in complete understanding. It was seven years ago that Germany had invaded Poland. No one at that time could imagine that act of aggression would turn into concentration camps and the mass executions of so many Jews. "If only…" was a recurring comment by so many intellectuals and politicians. I enlisted because the greatness of this country lay in the recognition there is no place for evil like that in this world.

I had no idea what I faced nor what it involved or would become. I recognized what it was.

"Whatever you need," Detective Melvin Baumgartner said as he placed his hand on mine.

Chapter Twenty-Two

It was late afternoon when the police inquiries ended. I realized I needed to face Dr. Kingsley and fully expected it to be an intellectual tennis match filled with verbal parley. In that regard, it would be safer than crossed sabers. I just hoped I was up to the task.

Mel was kind enough to let me use his office phone while he stepped out. It was one of those occasions when he didn't want to know what he probably already knew. I found Kingsley's number in the directory and dialed. I heard the phone pick up. A span of about fifteen seconds of silence ensued before any kind of recognition.

"Yes?" The voice was recognizable.

"Dr. Kingsley, this is Harold Bergman. I believe I have some news for you regarding Wilhelm Bradenhorst."

"Impressive, Mr. Bergman. And so quickly. What is it exactly?"

"I think it would be prudent to discuss this in person. Is there somewhere we can meet?"

"There are so few places of which I am an habitue. Would you consider coming to my residence?"

I graciously accepted his invitation when I considered it was the place where I could learn the most about him. He set a time of seven in the evening. It was already four. I needed to stop by the Carnegie Library before it closed.

The look on my face could probably be described as frenzied. It was largely due to time more than any type of ailment. Karla found me at the front desk as my head bobbed left to right and back again.

"Breathe. It's good for you." There was likely some concern amid her sarcasm.

I blurted out the name 'Christophe Blanc' and indicated an address. My hope is she would be able to find any kind of smattering of info before the library closed. I stressed I did not need an entire dossier, just a glimmer of understanding about the man in hopes I could speculate on the rest using reasonable lines of logic. At this point, that was about all I could conveniently do.

What she was able to determine within a scant forty-five minutes was date of birth (April 16, 1890); graduated from the University of Paris in 1910; had encounters with Marie Curie through the Pasteur Institute despite specializing in chemistry; was initially drafted by the French army in 1914 but became a medic; removed from that position by the General Staff in 1915 and reassigned to the explosives division alongside Victor Grignard. It was a lot of information to absorb in a brief period, especially as Karla spoke at a rapid pace and referenced French names in a decidedly Kansas accent.

A doctor, a banker, an engineer, and a chemist. In my head I heard all the makings of a nursery rhyme. Either that or the pieces of a potential criminal organization. Wild theories aside, it still offered no indication of William Johnson's lost time, only that certain possibilities existed. My fear was this could become a wild goose chase. Ghost stories are often derived from the smatterings of a few truthful anecdotes.

The one thing I hadn't noticed as I perused Kingsley's home was the iron gate in front of the main driveway. While there were two doors that locked in the middle and would open wide, I discovered a smaller pedestrian gate close to the brick wall. When I approached it, I discovered an intercom with a buzzer, similar to what you would find in most apartments. I pressed the button right at seven.

"Mr. Bergman?" the tinny voice came back.

"Yes."

"Please." His one-word response was followed by a clicking sound that seemed to unlock the gate. I entered and closed the door behind me.

The massive oak front door was well over six feet tall with small windows at the very top. It would take someone of Goliath's height to even gaze out. Or, for that matter, peer in. Another intercom and buzzer were just outside the front door. I pressed it. This time I was wordlessly allowed entry.

I found no way to accurately gauge the size or scope of the house as it was well hidden behind a brick wall and clouded by mature adult trees. The front foyer was not grand like Versailles but did have a marble-tiled floor and solid staircase to the right which held thick carpeting. The hallway in front of me ran into the house to what I presumed was a dining room and kitchen. The lack of light made it merely speculation. I could clearly see the parlor to my left. Through silk-curtained French doors, I walked into a room that could only be described as Medieval in décor. The fireplace was large enough to roast the proverbial fatted cow while the wide marble mantle displayed ornate sculptures, most of which seemed foreign to me. There were small tapestries on either wall of the fireplace, several coats of arms throughout, a few crystal candlesticks, a full-sized suit of armor in the corner, along with a combination radio and Victrola that was a good twenty years out of fashion. Everything appeared as though it were from a lost time in history. It could have been an homage to the dead and dying.

Dr. Kingsley sat in one of the two large wing-backed chairs that bookended the fireplace, a large brandy snifter gently held like a newborn child, swirled in a delicate fashion. He had a look of utter satisfaction and ease on his face. With what was yet to be determined.

"Adet Vintage Cognac. 1940. I have less than a case left. I am quite certain the Germans drank or destroyed the rest. As to the former, they likely had very little palate where this was concerned. And to the latter, what one cannot possess one often destroys." He took in a whiff, then looked at me as though he suddenly realized I was there. "Would you care for some?"

I held my hand like a traffic cop, allowed him to gloat in his complacency, and sat in the other chair.

"I hope I'm not interrupting anything, doctor."

"I had just completed a celebratory repast for my birthday and was finishing it off with splendor."

"I certainly do not want to intrude on your festivities."

"Nonsense. Especially if you have news for me."

The story I presented to him indicated I made brief mention of this German con man to my acquaintances on the force who fortuitously advised me of the discovery of the body. I left out the part where I was the cause of the discovery. I described nothing further. An empty trap will sometimes draw a willing prey.

"Have they ascertained the cause of death?" His demeanor was almost blasé, as though he wasn't concerned one way or another, mostly inquisitive as a man of science in spite of his financial loss.

"They believe he was poisoned."

The glass swirled, the deep amber liquid came up the sides to coat it, the hand that held it giving the warmth it deserved.

"And what are your thoughts on the matter?"

"I didn't have any. I came here to collect yours."

He looked at me as though he knew what he wanted to say but simply waited for the opportune moment to say it.

"How does one become a private detective, Mr. Bergman?"

His question caught me off guard completely.

"I was a policeman before the war."

"Drafted?"

"Enlisted."

"But you didn't return to the police department?"

"No."

"Why not?"

"I guess you could say my sense of justice became skewed."

While he didn't exactly lean forward, his shoulders moved ever so slightly. Something I said caught his attention.

"How so?" he inquired matter-of-factly.

"The idea that atrocities occur within the scope of a patriotic obligation to curb the spread of evil. I just wondered how a country can use the thing it is fighting to eradicate it."

"Without becoming that thing," he said, as though

finishing my thought. “Yes, I appreciate your dilemma.” He continued to swirl the glass. I figured there was a purpose to it but it started to annoy me. “Would you be willing to take up the challenge of Mr. Bradenhorst’s death?”

“I’d prefer to leave that matter to the police.”

“Understandable. Then let me ask you this. Might I assume there is a possibility Mr. Bradenhorst might have been killed by someone else he had taken advantage of?”

My heart skipped a bit as I thought about Sharon and Martin Kaye and how that turned out. I concluded the investment story was a phony given all the myriad coincidences that flew around. I didn’t give much credence to Kingsley as the killer given the sparsity of time in the apartment and the lack of benefit in doing so, yet I couldn’t rule anything out.

“Given your description of him, that is a reasonable assumption.”

“Would you be so kind as to keep me abreast of the investigation?”

“I can give you the lead detective’s name and phone number.”

He shook his head, a slight almost comical smile on his face.

“I am not interested in establishing any kind of relationship with the local gendarmes. You, on the other hand, impress me as a man of integrity and virtue. The kind who is more concerned with a sense of balance and equilibrium.”

Although the nature of the words should have come across like a compliment, the way they were spoken seemed almost like an accusation. To me, he described an individual who was headstrong and resolute, perhaps even uncompromising. It seemed opposite of one with integrity.

I felt almost dizzy, breathless, as though an aspect of the room created a hypnotic effect in an effort to make me acquiesce to an unknown request. I nodded and stood if only to get my blood flowing.

"I'll contact you if I learn anything further."

He did not get up, did not offer a departing handshake, but just kept swirling the glass. I turned and started to leave the room. A coat of arms to the right of the French doors caught my eye, the inscription something I knew I needed to remember.

The first thing I did when I stepped outside was breathe. I took in the evening air deeply within my lungs, like a doughboy in France who tried to expel the foul gases that invaded my body. It was twilight when I came to this house. A brief thirty minutes later it was dark. It was as though an entire lifetime passed. I wondered if William Johnson had the same feeling. I pondered if he visited with Kingsley and just didn't admit to it. Or perhaps couldn't.

That one parlor was a place lost in time. It wasn't Wichita and it wasn't 1946 just after the war. It was a world I could only imagine. As my lightheadedness started to fade, I could only wonder if I imagined any of it or all of it.

I walked briskly. I had parked my car across the street, not as far as when I had done reconnaissance earlier. Once seated inside, I gripped the steering wheel. Had I held on to keep from falling over or simply try to convince myself it was real? I breathed in deeply, then out, then in again. I needed to leave as quickly as possible. Movement was life. I started the car and put it into gear.

I turned left onto North Thirteenth Street and headed west. I drove slowly. I intended to look around and validate my surroundings. I tried to make sure everything was real. I turned south onto North Topeka Street. A brief thought entered my mind as I passed St. Francis Hospital. I realized I needed to go home.

I parked in the back alley in the spot my dear landlady Constance Hanover designated for me. I said her name in my mind. I recited the names of the other residents. I quickly remembered the last time I saw them and what we talked about. I wanted them to continue to be real to me.

I quietly entered the building. I did not want to arouse anyone's attention or to have a conversation with anyone. After I entered my apartment and locked the door, I turned to see my wonderful feline companions, Sir Pounce and Lady Mittens, and got on the floor to rub their bellies and scratch their ears and talk to them lovingly as I would an infant. It took every ounce of strength to get myself up again.

I drank glass after glass of water. What I understood was my brief encounter with Dr. Douglas Price Kingsley was unlike my association with Albert Whitman or Alan Isbell or even the late Sylvia Morgan-Smith. This was not the stench of impropriety by someone of extreme wealth. This was entirely different and unknown. A darkness that somehow seeped into my pores.

Then it dawned on me, the image that caught my eye as I departed. The coat of arms of two crossed lightning bolts with a five-pointed star in the crest. And the writing at the bottom of the shield:

Tenemus fulgur.

I found an envelope and wrote it down quickly. I stumbled into the bedroom and fell into the bed, clothes and shoes and all.

Chapter Twenty-Three

When I had awoken at the 110th Evac Hospital, it was a week before New Year's Eve of 1944. The last memory I had was of the heavy fighting around Stavelot. Shells landed everywhere. Bullets whizzed by like angry mosquitos. When our engineers couldn't blow up the bridge over the River Ambleve, the *Kampfgruppe* Peiper entered the town. During the retreat was when I got shot in the calf and foot. I limped my way as far as I could with comrades before I fell into a swirling darkness.

The morphine dulled my head as well as the pain. I sensed I was no longer in Belgium. There were vague dreams of bantam car testing at Pope Army Airfield just outside Fayetteville; Kellie and Allison and Dianne in the PX; and my dances with Emily and Lauren at USO events. Names but no faces. It seemed like ancient history. But in that hospital bed, I recognized the uniforms enough to know I was in good hands but didn't know where. I vaguely overheard plans to ship me off the 15th General Hospital all the way north in Liege but it was bombed on Thanksgiving and only now recovering.

Words swirled around in piecemeal. Even though they were English, I grasped for meaning. Too many groggy nights. I needed surgery. Foot shot bad. Might never walk again. Careful for infection. Amputation unlikely, but still a possibility.

The meeting with Kingsley was strangely similar. Surrounded by two felines who simply stared at me offered no explanation. I drew aside the curtains and let in the morning light. The Baby Ben on the table next to my bed showed just after 9:30. My clothes were rumpled, and my mouth was dry like I had chewed on an old sock. My nose was stuffy and a dull throb reverberated in my temples, rhythms that Gage Brewer might appreciate.

I made a pot of coffee, fed Lady Mittens and Sir Pounce, and splashed more cold water in my face. The urge to immediately take a hot shower was set aside. I did not want to be relaxed but rather invigorated. I needed to shake off the malaise of the last twelve hours and prevent any memory from disappearing completely.

I was dismayed to consider that I was as near death from an interview with a possible suspect as when fighting the Germans in Belgium. The infantry could not be considered a paragon of social interaction. Yet there was the remembrance of strange sensations while simply engaging in conversations.

I recalled Kingsley swirl his snifter as one would do to enjoy a fine brandy or cognac. I could not picture him ever taking a sip or so much as bringing it up to savor its aroma. Why? Then it hit me. The muted scent of sage, as though I were in a forest within that sitting room. It weighed heavy on my lungs, pressed me down, as though Kingsley himself stepped on my chest even though he sat relatively still in his chair and never moved once. Except for that hand with the glass.

Nothing that was said had any air of subtext or alluded to a deeper meaning than an inquiry into a possible murder investigation. Except for a vague compliment that seemed out of place. *You, on the other hand, impress me as a man of integrity and virtue. The kind who is more concerned with a sense of balance and equilibrium.* Someone would refer to 'justice' or even 'righteousness' if they were intent on the apprehension of a killer. What 'balance' and 'equilibrium' meant were beyond me.

Like a feather that fell from a tree, I finally noticed the envelope upon which I wrote what was ostensibly a Latin phrase. *Tenemus fulgur.* Given its placement on a coat of arms, I doubted it was part of a Catholic Mass. I knew a gentleman who would likely provide some reasonable answer, though it might take some doing to get him to enunciate it.

Professor Bryce Horne taught Ancient History and Languages at Wichita University. However, I knew Bradley Wolrebinski used him to inquire about arcane subjects that were within his scope of knowledge though not regularly taught to impressionable students. Professor Horne was tall and slender with eyebrows that were as white and bushy as his hair. A large bulbous nose was prominent on a face covered in countless wrinkles. He was wildly energetic but exhibited difficulty focusing on one subject at a time.

"Yes, yes," he said to my translation inquiry. "Latin indeed. Absolutely."

"What does it mean, professor?"

"We hold the lightning."

I stared at him and he at me. He quickly became flustered.

"I'm almost positive of that," he continued as he reached for a large book, opened it, and flipped madly through the pages. "Yes, yes. I was correct."

"Do you know of any coat of arms who would have that as their motto?"

He raised a finger as though to indicate awareness of the answer but words did not come out of his mouth. Instead, he moved like a squirrel toward a large floor-to-ceiling bookcase in his office and used the same finger to pinpoint three equally large books. He removed them from the shelves and carried them like a baby to the desk where he practically threw them down, likely from their weight. He started to open each one to specific pages as though by memory while he finally issued forth a recitation.

"The expression has been used in one fashion or another by various esoteric groups. There is one known as Gabalisians who follow the precepts of the fictional Comte de Gabalis from the text of the same name by Abbe Nicolas-Pierre-Henri de Montfaucon de Villars. A very close approximation of that expression, *fulgur impius ferit,* 'lightning strikes the wicked', is the dictum of the Order of the Dawn of York, an off-shoot of the Hermetic Order of the Golden Dawn, whose philosophy was based primarily on the Hermetic Qabbalah, while the Dawn of York was more akin to Sufism."

"You said Kabbalah?"

He spelled it out with a Q, then proceeded to explain this was more closely tied to Christian Cabalistic theology. The intellectual waters started to rise and nearly drowned me. I became overwhelmed by a tidal wave of historical information that gushed forth in an overwhelming fashion. Professor Horne was definitely the person to come to, but I would need to attend a semester's worth of classes to fully comprehend the repercussions. Time was definitely not on my side.

I borrowed a sheet of paper and took notes on specific aspects of some of these esoteric groups. It was apparent some deep thought was involved in the creation of these orders, each with their own distinctive sacraments and purposes. I couldn't imagine what the purpose was for these organizations. Then I remembered an encounter with a young man in boot camp who was not particularly religious. He asked why people went to church or temple, considered it a waste of time, and hoped to achieve whatever success he could in life through his own means. It occurred to me that folks believe most in what gives them the greatest comfort or will provide them with the means to achieve it.

As I started to leave, Professor Horne went on another tangent.

"Beyond all of these arcane philosophies, the largest beliefs concern Sir Francis Bacon, who many believe to have been the true author of the works of Shakespeare. He was a bona fide polymath, perhaps the greatest of all time. Many Theosophists believe Bacon faked his own death on April 9, 1626, and eventually became an Ascended Master some fifty-eight years later under the name Saint Germaine."

"But to what end?"

"Supreme power. The ability to exert control."

"Over what?"

"Anything. Everything. Whatever his heart desired."

This was no comic book like Superman. History books told stories of groups whose belief systems were far more extraordinary than any religion I knew of. I understood what Catholics and Protestants and Jews believed and accepted, could fathom what their moral tenets were, and accept the intention of their rites and rituals. This brief time with Professor Horne made me realize a greater evil existed than the criminals from the streets or unscrupulous wealthy businessmen whose lives were guided by greed. I read the Old Testament countless times, studied the Talmud when I could, worked as a policeman, and faced a dire enemy in the war. Despite all of that I could not fathom the darkness that I now had to consider.

I repeated the phrase over and over in my head. *Tenemus fulgur*. "We hold the lightning." I could not connect it to an ethos or other belief system. I finally heard it in my head. *Tenemus.* 'Tin mouse.' *Fulgur.* 'Vulgar.' William Johnson had the expression 'vulgar tin mouse' in his head for no apparent reason. I saw it in Dr. Douglas Kingsley's parlor. Johnson saw it there, too. His lost time could now be accounted for. But to what end?

At this point, I needed to feel grounded in my religion, given what I heard for the past hour so distinctly outside of my world. I hoped Bradley would provide some comfort, but I speculated deep down the artistic nature of Svetlana would connect me to what I needed to hold onto.

It was just after noon when I reached their beautiful Victorian house on Park Place. I knocked solidly on the heavy oak door. Svetlana greeted me in a paint-covered smock as she held a brush and rag to wipe it off.

"I would kiss you," she said, "but your face would have a mauve smear on it."

Her off-beat comment put a smile on my face. She called, or rather yelled, into the house for her husband. Bradley approached me in the foyer.

"Boychik," he bellowed as he grabbed my head and

kissed me on both cheeks. “Come in. I was just making a brisket sandwich. You want me to make you one?”

We sat in the kitchen at a small table, the two of us with large brisket sandwiches and a sour dill pickle while Svetlana sipped her tea. I came across as unusually quiet given my past interactions with them always raised my level of energy.

“Is the Kabbalah evil?” I asked sheepishly. They looked at each other in uncertain silence.

“Why do you ask?” Bradley questioned softly, a very atypical tone for him.

“The Kabbalah is a set of teachings that explain the relationship between the eternal God and the mortal universe. Because it is a more mystical interpretation of the Bible and Talmud, there are many who cannot grasp its significance. People will refer to things they do not understand as evil.” Svetlana was clear and precise in her description. It was indicative of a woman who created landscapes both with a paint brush and with flowers.

“What about true evil?” I asked in return.

“It gives itself away every time.” Bradley had an impish smile.

“Perhaps in your books,” I responded.

“Ah, but look at Albert Whitman and Alan Isbell,” Bradley countered. “Evil has the unenviable trait of believing in its own supremacy. The unmitigated gall to assume it can’t fail because it is more powerful than its adversary. But all it takes is one minor flaw and its foundation weakens and falters. As you have said, this is what I write about.”

Svetlana reached out and touched my hand. Without castigating Bradley for his perceived dismissiveness, she searched my eyes for the meaning behind my inquiry.

I spent the next half hour telling them everything from the first discussion with William Johnson on Sunday evening to the information I got from Professor Horne. I presented them with every detail possible. This progressed beyond a criminal inquiry. It showed every indication of the most nefarious scheme since the war. I relied upon my experience as a policeman, my profound faith, and the love of my family and friends to assist in my capacity as a private investigator. If even the smallest portion of this inquiry was akin to what I learned within the last day, I could not imagine what further tools I would need to fight an evil this monstrous.

"So the people shouted when the priests blew with their trumpets; and it came to pass, when the people heard the sound of the trumpet, and the people shouted with a great shout, that the wall fell down flat, so that the people went up into the city, every man straight before him, and they took the city."

The pride of Joshua 6:20 made my heart beat strongly through my chest. Svetlana spoke as eloquently as a rabbi.

"Let me make some inquiries," Bradley said, more in his usual brusqueness. "I know some people who, while not necessarily criminal in nature, have what you might call alternate views on how things should be."

"I don't want to jeopardize either of you," I said in a rather pleading tone.

"You shouldn't worry, Harold." I never quite knew Bradley's complete background except the tidbits he revealed during late night chess matches over schnapps. But when he instructed me not to worry, I felt strangely at peace.

It was time for me to update William Johnson.

Chapter Twenty-Four

It was midafternoon, just past the lunch hour so I was relatively sure I would find Mr. Johnson in his office. Mrs. Gallison saw me almost like radar and approached me before anyone else knew of my presence. Without even a mention of what I needed, she motioned to follow her to Johnson's office. A brief knock and then she opened the door. I turned to her before she closed it.

"No calls for the time being, Mrs. Gallison."

She nodded.

William Johnson looked as though he hadn't slept in a while. I didn't consider him to be the physically fit type but, in this instance, he had bags under his eyes and slouched shoulders. His face was even more pale than a man who spent most of his time indoors. Perhaps the dreams were more frightening than lack of sleep.

"I believe you had dinner on Friday evening with Dr. Douglas Price Kingsley."

He was non-plussed.

"If you say so. But how can you be sure?"

I advised him of my meeting at Kingsley's residence and the coat of arms.

"The Latin phrase is highly unique and your recollection of it fits. Do you recall the scent of sage?"

He let out a silent gasp that accompanied a look akin to an epiphany.

"Yes," he said strongly. "But I still have no

recollection of dinner nor anything after the late afternoon on Friday."

"Let's hold off on that for a moment. Since the beginning of the week, have you approved any significant loans or arranged any noteworthy business deals for the bank?"

"No."

"Call in Mrs. Gallison."

The intercom snapped on and off. The dutiful secretary entered in less than fifteen seconds.

"Mrs. Gallison, what bank business has Mr. Johnson been directly involved with since the Monday of this week?"

She looked back and forth between me and her boss. Perhaps it was to gain approval to answer or understand why Johnson couldn't answer that question for himself.

"There was a brief unscheduled meeting with Mr. Hobart Brady of the Chamber of Commerce and a loan approval for a small business," she said efficiently.

I looked at Johnson. He was perplexed. By the look on his face, I could tell he had no recollection of either event.

"Tell me more about this loan."

"Give me just a moment."

She stepped outside, ostensibly to secure a file or the paperwork. William Johnson sat in a daze. When Mrs. Gallison returned, she indicated a gentleman named Damiano Alemagna secured a small business loan in the amount of one thousand dollars. He was an engineer formerly with Cessna and hoped to build lightweight aircraft at a more economical rate for other small businesses. The dollar amount seemed almost negligible in terms of what would be needed to establish such a venture given the details as outlined in the application.

"References?"

"Management personnel at Cessna attested to his competence and educational background."

"Any personal references?"

"Only one. Christophe Blanc. His occupation is listed as Chemist."

It felt like a sharp knife pierced my throat.

"When was the application made?"

"Monday the ninth."

"And approved?"

"The sixteenth. This past Monday."

I thanked her for her efficiency. When the questions ceased, she left the office. At that moment, William Johnson clutched his head in his hands. What I gathered was a normally sedate man seemed to be in shambles, all traces of normalcy and sanity wiped clean as though he had a completely new personality.

"This is bad. This is bad." He repeated the phrase until it became a whisper. He took one giant breath and exhaled before he looked at me with tears in his eyes. "What does it all mean?"

I had no more understanding but knew enough to not simply leave him more fearful due to our combined ignorance. The best I could do was present a reasonable supposition in as logical a fashion as possible.

"I can connect Kingsley to Bradenhorst and Blanc. This Alemagna is also connected to Blanc. And then there is Bradenhorst who knew a Dewey Purcell, another British man. We've got five European men, all in some kind of professional field, all with specific identifiable professional backgrounds. However, there is nothing definitive to connect them more than in an ephemeral way. Kingsley seems to have various esoteric interests, but I haven't discovered any group or cult of that sort to pin him to." I gasped as I ran out of breath. "I have some connections in the FBI for a matter of this scope." I didn't want to reach out to Dorothy Martin unless it was absolutely necessary.

"No, please. You can't do that," Johnson implored. "I have every faith in you, Mr. Bergman. Both your skill and your discretion. I can't afford, the bank can't afford even the slightest odor of impropriety."

"But as far as I can tell, you haven't done anything wrong."

"It is really all about appearances. Someone could easily fault my character for allowing whatever this is to happen. I can't recall this meeting with Kingsley or the approval of the loan to Alemagna. Such things could set a dangerous precedent. This would be seen as a weakness, a character trait unacceptable in financial sectors."

It dawned on me this bank and his professional standing was all this man had left. He had no spouse, no semblance of a social life nor even a desire to have one. Everything in his life revolved around his arrival and departure from the bank. Without it, he might not have a viable reason to live.

I started to feel bad for him until I realized I could easily become that way. I certainly had more close friends, like King Mar, and my relationship with Eileen. My father and the temple were strongholds in my life. Yet this evolution into an investigator, whether private of for the insurance company, became a deep focus in my life. I could see how easy it would be to wear blinders and shut out all the other good things in my life and lose them for the sake of a single-minded pursuit.

I found no reason to continue that train of thought for now. What I needed to do was focus on the pieces of this puzzle and how they might fit together. Beyond that, I needed to determine how William Johnson fit in. It couldn't be for a simple small business loan. A well-planned bank robbery could secure far more capital. What was the scent of sage? Did it cover something, perhaps an intoxicant that might have hypnotized both myself and Johnson?

I instructed Johnson to have the bank records scoured for references to the five gentlemen we were aware of, either as clients or indications of any other association, no matter how slight. Without the FBI as a resource, I was limited to Karla Duggan and the Carnegie Library as well as the secretive interests of Bradley and Svetlana. Though I had doubts, I was inclined to believe this was significantly important.

Karla Duggan sat with me in a back room while we perused three months' worth of the newspaper. For now, my focus was on reference to do with banking or aircraft. I couldn't be certain how broad of a search to make.

August 18—Eleven planes were damaged at the Arther airport after it was struck by a twister during a violent thunderstorm. It appeared the storm was localized and had no impact anywhere else in the vicinity.

September 1—With contributions from Beech and Cessna, construction was to begin on a new wind tunnel at Wichita University. This was significant from an educational standpoint, but who else would benefit from its completion, or if said construction were prevented?

September 10—A report of the death of Norris J

Stone, owner and founder of the Stone Propeller Manufacturing Company. Nothing appeared unusual in his passing on the surface.

Without understanding its importance, the wind tunnel did not seem significant, unless the research associated with it had ancillary benefits elsewhere. There were many small aircraft companies to consider the passing of a businessman to be impactful, unless Stone's background was significant. The airport, however, located in the 2800 block of West Pawnee, intrigued me. A small obscure location for planes could be a possibility for unscrupulous means. Or did these professional gentlemen have the means to control the weather, especially given the nature of the storm?

I saw Karla with a serious look reading an article. I cleared my throat to get her attention I had to do that a couple of times before it worked.

"Banking or aircraft?" I asked.

"Neither."

"What then?"

"I'm reading about the passing of S.M. Stevens, quote, one of Wichita's early West Side Syrian merchants, unquote. One of the pioneers in dry goods and groceries. And then, not satisfied with that, he started a wholesale tobacco business in 1922 which he operated until just a couple of years ago. And one of his sons is an army colonel currently in Paris."

"This city has a lot of significant pioneers. We need to stay focused on banking because of Johnson, and aircraft because that is the biggest industry."

"Why?" She had a blank look of doubt or uncertainty. I couldn't tell which.

"What do you mean 'Why'? Didn't I explain how

important this was?"

"No. I mean the part about staying focused on those two things." She put down her paper and leaned forward. "I've known you a long time. When it comes to this private eye shtick, you're good. Really good. Like, better than Humphrey Bogart good. But that's only when it comes to criminals. All this stuff you've been telling me does not sound like some Jimmy Cagney gangster. 'Come out and take it, you yellow-bellied rat or I'll give it to you through the door.' Your doctor pal is educated and probably never fired any kind of weapon. If you just focus on two things, you'll miss the train."

Everything she said made sense, but I didn't have the kind of mind to think of any way other than a policeman would. Nothing in my training or education as a Jew prepared me for the deepest and darkest aspects of these circumstances. Yet I was aware of them, knew something to be going on that could undermine everything I held dear. If I didn't stand up to it, who would?

I asked her to once again look into anything associated with any of the five men, whether in the United States or Europe. My thoughts drifted to the almost hypnotic feeling I had when I visited Dr. Kingsley and the coat of arms. 'We hold the lightning' contained a profound message. Something as unpredictable and deadly that could be held and maintained, perhaps even controlled, implied a person or persons willing to use whatever powers available to them for whatever purpose they desired. A doctor, a banker, an architect, a chemist, and an engineer. All from Europe. All of an age approximate to being relatively young men during the First World War. Likely influenced or impacted by its brutality. Perhaps even demoralized by it.

Then again, the atrocities of the most recent war, especially what was reported to have been perpetrated against the Jewish population of Europe, were, at least to me, a greater crime against humanity. The trials in Nuremberg went on at this time. The laws of international courts would come to bear upon real war criminals. While I tried to stay aware of what went on, it angered me far too much. I could only hope the results would once and for all put an end to such brutality.

Then, suddenly, for a brief moment, a surge of defiance and a strength of conviction arose within me. I wanted to take action against the Nazi cowards who brutally murdered those who they deemed inferior only because they had the power and resources to do so. What if I held the power over them? I contemplated how many were not currently on trial, how many monsters escaped Germany and, subsequently, escaped justice.

My heart raced. A bit of sweat appeared on my forehead. I had no idea where such virulent thoughts came from and how they could take over my more rational sensibilities. For now, I returned to a more normal state for me. It felt the same as when I first left Dr. Kingsley's house, breathed in fresh air and expunged my lungs of a stale and toxic contaminant.

It fit together like a jigsaw puzzle. A chemist and a doctor. The scent of sage. A swirling brandy snifter. William Johnson losing nearly two days of his life as though he were asleep. As though he were under anesthesia.

It wasn't a puzzle that came together. It was a fog that lifted. The beginning of the clarity. I needed to shake off the lingering dread of doubt and realize yet again I had the strength to succeed.

It was time to find a doctor to advise me on how to determine what secrets were hidden in the sage and how to avoid the hallucinatory effects. I needed to dream my own dreams and not those of the evil ones in our midst.

Chapter Twenty-Five

There were two things unusual about the knock on my door at just past eight in the morning. Both of them involved Bradley Wolrebinski. First, this was far earlier than I had ever known him to be awake. He and Svetlana were night owls, prone toward finding their greatest creativity after the sun set. The other thing was I never encountered him outside of his home or a social engagement of one kind or another in all the years I had known him. While I was a welcome guest in their home, there was never a mention of my abode outside of references to the cats. His appearance confused and concerned me more than it pleased me.

The cats roamed about as I awakened and opened the pocket doors. They were intrigued by the big man with the coiffured beard and moustache and circled his feet as though he were their parent. He smiled and rubbed both their heads. At that point they scurried to the cupboard to await their morning meal.

"I'm sorry to disturb you at this hour," he said graciously and rather quieter than I was used to. Bradley was a man of big appetites who enjoyed the interplay of words and the intellectual discourse that came with it. His tone was one of apology.

"Let me get changed and I'll make some coffee," I said in reference to my pajamas.

"No need."

We sat, he on the chair that barely held him and me on the loveseat. The cats remained at their location. It was silent for a bit, a rather perplexing feeling to say the least. Perhaps the lull before the storm.

"Is there something wrong, Bradley?"

"There very well could be." He stopped and composed himself. "A little over twenty years ago, a man I knew very briefly in Boston extended an invitation to join a group that formed in England. It was the remnants of an international pacifist group that arose after the end of the Great War. Their original intention was to advocate peaceful resolutions to political conflicts to prevent another global military action. Given the catastrophic nature of that war, they were noble intentions to say the least."

"Boston? What were you doing at the time?"

"I was in another field, not yet having started my writing career." His deferred response added to my curiosity about him. It seemed the answer might not be germane to the story. "This group decided their actions of the prior eight years had not been sufficient enough. There was some rather deep consideration they were an utter failure. The Irish Civil War, the Russian Civil War, the Greco-Turkish War. Now, while those were all mostly geographically regional, none of them could be circumvented due in some small measure to a sense of tribalism. The results are now part of historical record. The implication was there needed to be sterner measures to control resources in order to limit the potential for these skirmishes and to prevent them from spreading, almost like a plague."

"What kind of measures did they consider?"

"I never found out," he said with a shake of his head.

"Why not?"

"The proposed date of the meeting was to be April 9, 1926. It was to take place at an inn on the corner of Arundel Street and Temple Place. I was struck by the very specificity of the date and the exactness of the location. It was then I realized the date was the three-hundredth anniversary of the death of Sir Francis Bacon and the location was in proximity to the old Arundel House where he died."

A small amount of sweat appeared on Bradley's forehead. Another first in my association with him.

"Please forgive me but I'm not following you."

Bradley then went into detail about Bacon's alleged connections to Rosicrucians and the Freemasons; that according to legend his death was faked; that his treatise *Instauratio Magna* was actually a coded guide to achieving great power through the application of the known physical sciences. As he saw it, the intention behind this current group was to exert control over global financial and industrial institutions for the purpose of creating a peaceful utopian society by limiting the resources required to wage war.

This fit what Professor Horne briefly educated me on. As confounding as all of this seemed, I now had two educated men intoning similar theories that surrounded arcane lore. I needed to pay attention and try as best as I could to comprehend the implications.

"Who was the man who approached you?"

"The banker, Dewey Purcell."

A chemist, a doctor, an engineer, an architect, and a banker. Professional fields that could reach into a plethora of industries. To what end? That was yet to be determined. Perhaps William Johnson's episode was a test. He had no recollection of his lost time nor of authorizing the nominal loan to Alemagna. Were this group to follow through on other people or businesses, they could exert influence over larger institutions, manipulate the stock market, guide industries to destroy weapons of war, or take complete control of the governments of various countries.

"There are only three of them now," I said with a degree of assurance.

"That you know of."

"You realize they have to be stopped."

"You can't stop them." Desperation oozed in his voice. He sounded almost defeated.

"*David said moreover, The Lord that delivered me out of the paw of the lion, and out of the paw of the bear, he will deliver me out of the hand of this Philistine.*" I believed it as surely as anything else. I was never injured as a policeman. I survived the horrors of war. I faced down men of wealth and power. How was this possible? Why would it be if not to be brought to a greater purpose? I had faith I could be victorious.

Bradley looked at me and gazed into my eyes in a way unlike any of our deepest conversations in the past. He was charged with the passion of our religion and returned to a fervent belief in the power of the Almighty. He took my hands in his and finished the verse.

"And Saul said unto David, Go, and the Lord be with thee."

I went to Wesley Medical Center to consult with Dr. Enders who treated me after my encounter with Jeremy Thatcher. Given my limited medical knowledge and not wishing to take up the good doctor's time, I had to be brief and specific, but not elaborate too much.

"Do you know of any drugs that could induce both memory loss as well as be used in hypnosis?"

His eyes went wide as he stared at me with a degree of uncertainty.

"Well, I suppose some anticholinergic might be used in such an application."

"You're gonna have to translate, doc."

"These are drugs used in surgical situations to reduce post-operative nausea and vomiting. One, scopolamine, was used as anesthesia around the turn of the century."

"Tell me more about this scopolamine."

"It's from the nightshade family. In higher doses, it can have a powerful hallucinogenic effect."

"Does it smell like sage?"

"No, not at all. In fact, sage would counter the amnesia effects of the scopolamine."

I started to get the idea of the lingo and tried to put a couple of ideas together.

"So, scopolamine in high doses can be hallucinogenic, but sage kind of balances it out."

"Correct, in a rather prosaic manner of speaking. No offense."

"None taken. So, if a scientist, or a surgeon, let's say, figured out the right balance, could it be used to hypnotize someone? Maybe give them an idea to do something but then forget about it?"

His face contorted as he considered the question.

"Theoretically, yes."

Dr. Enders indicated the administration of the drug was via intravenous. Consequently, the whole thing fell apart because neither Johnson or I were in a doctor's office and received an injection. I didn't inquire about

Johnson but I knew I didn't have anything to drink. So, how did it get into me, this magical drug I speculatively created out of scientific thin air? There was no problem with the notion that, between a chemist and a surgeon, both highly qualified in their fields, such an elixir could be created. The only thing remained as to its delivery.

"One final thing, Dr. Enders? Can scopolamine, or any such combination of drugs, get into a person by any means other than injection? Perhaps a gas of some kind?"

"I can only limit my response to the known drugs from the hyoscine family, Mr. Bergman. Scopolamine exists solely as a liquid or powder. I know of no instance where it has been vaporized."

"Okay, then a powder. Let's say you got it on your hands."

"Certainly. But that would take upwards of four hours for complete efficacy. As it is designed for anesthesia or post-operative relief, the only viable methods of administration are intradermal or oral." He stopped, then appeared as though he considered other options. "Naturally, this hypothetical concoction might have other applications and concurrent side effects of which we have no knowledge. Given your scenario, that is."

The possibilities existed. Unfortunately, the only way to find out was to meet with Kingsley again and pay particular attention to everything around him. However, my earlier story would not hold water again. Our last meeting had the earmarks of finality. I started to lose my grip on this the more I realized the darkness of it.

I stopped by the station to look for Mel Baumgartner. I already had information from one doctor.

Now, I needed to know what Dr. Gerhardt discovered with regard to the death of Wilhelm Bradenhorst.

Mel pulled me into an empty office almost on the q.t. His concern for my wellbeing needed to be balanced with his position on the force.

"I take it you're looking for the report on Bradenhorst," he said, almost in a whisper.

"I am."

"Autopsy report is not final but there is a preliminary. I'll get it. You wait here."

He left quickly, somewhat reminding me of Red Skelton from "I Dood It." It was a rather bizarre appearance from a seasoned police officer.

He came back just as quickly with a folder that contained several pages. He referred only to the top page.

"Stomach contained trace amounts of disulfur dichloride."

"Mustard gas," I blurted out.

"Really?"

"Yeah."

"Then there's this. 'Stomach lining shows signs of long-term scarring and prior gastrointestinal bleeding.' Was that from the poison?" he asked aloud.

"No. My guess is this guy had an ulcer, and he ingested an agent he thought, or was told, would help his pain. Instead, it killed him."

"You said that Dr. Kingsley wasn't in that building for more than a minute."

"Less. He could have been delivering this so-called medicine."

"Which wasn't medicine but was poison."

Once again, an example of a chemist and a physician in cahoots.

"Thanks, Mel."

I started to walk out but he grabbed me, forcefully enough that it could almost be considered police brutality.

"Listen, Harold. This isn't the kind of stuff you should mess around with."

"Mel, have you ever backed down from a criminal? Given up an investigation?"

"No," he replied quietly, like a castigated child.

"I can't let this go."

I left quickly, as much to avoid a deeper discussion as to not lose my resolve. This was like the war all over again. You knew who the enemy was. You might even know where they were. The thing you had to figure was how to attack them. What I needed was a bite to eat.

I was of a mind to invite Eileen for a nosh and try to get my mind off this spider web. Then I realized that was the last thing I should do. I knew I needed a bit of tranquility. The back booth at the Pan American Café would do perfectly.

I was cordial with King Mar, told him I was on a case that I couldn't describe for the time being, inquired about his well-being, and then settled into an open-faced hot roast beef sandwich and a cup of coffee. The warmth and substance of the meal rejuvenated me, made me feel alive after I dealt with so much death.

As the air cleared inside my head, King Mar looked at me from the front counter while he spoke on the phone. He had a concerned look on his face. He put the phone down and walked with determined steps toward me.

"There's a man on phone, says he wants to talk to you. I tried to tell you're not here. He don't believe me.

Says he knows you are."

"Who is it?"

"Said it's your doctor."

Neither Dr. Enders nor Dr. Gerhardt could be considered my doctor. Besides, if it were one of them, they certainly would have identified themselves. I wiped my mouth with a napkin and followed King Mar to the front.

"Mr. Bergman, I'm sorry to disturb you at dinner."

I recognized Kingsley's voice. I should have been concerned that he knew exactly where I was and what I was doing. It was all a magician's trick. By this time, it was old hat.

"Not at all."

"I'd like to see you again, if it wouldn't be a bother."

"Well, Dr. Kingsley, as I stated earlier, I'm not all that interested in looking into Bradenhorst's death as the police have that matter well in hand."

"Oh, do they?" He sounded dubious. "How nice for them. However, this is an entirely different matter, Mr. Bergman. A business proposition that I believe, in the brief time we have spoken, is well suited to your temperament and skills. It has the potential to be both highly lucrative and extremely rewarding."

"In that case, I suppose it would be judicious to offer you some of my time."

"I should say so. Shall we say seven tomorrow evening at my home?"

"I'll be there with bells on.'

Then the king commanded, and they brought Daniel, and cast him into the den of lions. Now the king spake and said unto Daniel, Thy God whom thou servest continually, he will deliver thee. A fancy house in

Riverside was the lion’s den. There would be no weapon beyond my wits and intelligence and faith to extricate me from that which would seek to do me harm. I prayed it was enough.

Chapter Twenty-Six

The United States infantry soldier was well equipped to go into battle: an M1 Garand rifle .30-06 with an M1 bayonet and scabbard; a Colt M1911 handgun; an M1923 cartridge belt, a bandolier with twelve five round clips; an M3 trench knife; anywhere from three to six Mk 2 grenades; an M1C helmet and M43 combat boots; an M1936 field bag; an M1942 first aid pouch; a canteen; K-rations. I went through boot camp and trained under some of the toughest drill instructors I could imagine. This was for the sole purpose of preparing men for battle against an enemy who had great resolve.

My time at the police academy, while not as intense, was detailed and organized. Our gear included boots, pants, shirt, leather jacket, a revolver, in my case a Smith and Wesson .38, truncheon, note pad and pencil, and ammunition belt. The organizations I worked for tried to prepare me for all known eventualities based on historical data and years of an organized system. Part of that training was to contemplate the unknown, to extrapolate possible scenarios by using the information available. The goal was to be able to respond to any circumstances in any conditions in as rapid a time frame as possible.

I could think of no viable reason for Dr. Kingsley to wish to see me. He was far too intelligent and cunning to honestly believe I could prove he had a hand in Bradenhorst's death or that he manipulated William Johnson in any fashion. Therefore, I was not a threat to be eliminated, unless a sense of paranoia put him ill at ease.

Could it possibly be that he wanted me to join him in whatever venture he was a part of? Certainly, if he knew my whereabouts at any given moment, he surely must have some sense of my integrity and moral standing. This pondering created a kind of titillation, an eagerness to hear what he had to say regardless of the consequences. With that in mind, I created a back-up plan.

I sat and wrote a long report on Saturday morning while I drank more cups of coffee than was usual for me. The cats didn't seem appeased by their morning food offering. Perhaps they were and simply upset I had not paid them sufficient attention. This report detailed from the beginning everything I did, every person I encountered, every speculation and suspicion, and a couple of possible conclusions. This made for better reading rather than as a viable investigative document. Nevertheless, it was important to note my actions and efforts. I folded this report, put it first in a business envelope and sealed it, then put the whole ball of wax in a manilla envelope and sealed that.

The last time I wrote out what you could call a lengthy insurance policy, I left it in the hands of my dear landlady, Mrs. Hanover. The implication behind it gave her great pause and greater concern. I did not want to put her through that again.

The Carnegie Library offered limited hours on Saturday. I got there near closing for the sole purpose of an extended and hopefully uninterrupted conversation with Karla Duggan. When she saw the extremely serious look on my face, she motioned me with a nod of her head toward her private office as she cleared out the stragglers. She found me as I sat upright, like a dutiful schoolchild.

"I can place Kingsley, Purcell, and Blanc in London sometime around March or April in 1926." She began with a degree of mature efficiency.

"I learned that as well."

"Bradenhorst appears to have been in Germany by the late 1920s and through the war. Alemagna was in Canada as of 1933 per an article about his joining a firm in Toronto and then in New York City in 1935. Similar article about joining an engineering firm. Seems rather innocuous if you ask me."

"That's the way they're trying to make it look."

She leaned forward. I pulled the envelope out of my jacket pocket and placed it in front of her.

"Okay, what's this? Your last will and testament? Bergman, you're scaring me."

I explained to her that I was about to meet with Kingsley that evening at his house and that I suspected something corrupt in nature. I could not avoid this as it would mean allowing these men to continue whatever they were doing; by the same token, I wasn't a hundred percent sure if I possessed the tools necessary to defeat them. The envelope contained all the information I ascertained to this moment and she was to turn it over to Detective Melvin Baumgartner if she did not hear from me in seventy-two hours.

She nodded, a kind of understanding and acquiescence, breathed deep and exhaled.

As I started to leave, she made a comment I never heard her say before.

"I'll pray for you."

That seemed like an appropriate course of action for me as well. What I didn't want was to get caught up in the atmosphere of the temple and perhaps an extended conversation which would deter me from my sacred mission. That is what it had become. What was it about David that convinced him he could take on Goliath? In the end, there is nothing palpable. Only the deeply held feeling the Lord is on your side, and you will be given the strength to see the battle through. At this point, however, I had even less than a sling and a stone.

I arrived at two minutes before seven, clicked on the console outside the gate, and was buzzed in without a word. Like King Henry knew, the game was afoot.

The scene was almost exactly as it had been on my first visit. Kingsley sat in his chair, as he swirled the snifter with almost balletic movements. The other chair, closest to the fireplace, awaited me. This time, because of my prior awareness, the faint aroma of sage was noticeable.

"I believe we can dispense with the subtleties, Mr. Bergman. We are both aware of each other's efforts to gain information about our respective biographies."

I never heard investigatory practices worded so delicately.

"So, you know a lot about me, and I know a little bit about you."

"Please do not denigrate your own abilities. Knowledge is one thing. Intuition is another. It is a more privileged characteristic. Take the medical profession. Once all the tests have been completed, it is the competent physician who makes a diagnosis based on experience and instinct. What conclusions have you come to?"

"Five European professionals conspired to force various countries into a position of pacifism to avoid a further global conflict. Obviously, you were not successful."

He laughed boisterously, almost like Sydney Greenstreet as Casper Gutman.

"No, not quite. Do you know the problem with pacifism, Mr. Bergman? It lacks imperative. It lacks musculature. It has no strength and no power. *Blessed are the peacemakers. Be not overcome with evil, but overcome evil with good. Love your enemies, do good to them which hate you.* Those were my feelings after the first global conflict. The problem was the embers of hatred kept burning. Smoldering. Waiting for new fuel to start another conflagration. In essence, there would be no peace. So, I turned my thoughts to the Old Testament. *Breach for breach, eye for eye, tooth for tooth: as he hath caused a blemish in a man, so shall it be done to him again.* You're familiar with that?"

"Leviticus 19:20. However, the next verse is *And he that killeth a beast, he shall restore it; and he that killeth a man, he shall be put to death.*"

"Exactly. Neither war nor peace is the solution to achieve global and eternal prosperity."

"Then what is, Dr. Kingsley?"

Silence overtook the room. I could almost hear the brownish liquid swirl in the snifter. A low-pitched hiss at first reminded me of a snake. The lights in the chandelier appeared dimmer than when I first entered.

"Those five European professionals of which you

spoke earlier determined the only recourse was to control the systems of government, industry, and finance in such a fashion as to make it impossible to seek out conflict. They looked back in time, four hundred years in fact, when men were scientists and artists and philosophers, all wrapped up into one. The prime example was Sir Francis Bacon."

Kingsley started to talk about Bacon's life and associations with secret societies. All the while he referred to five European professionals as though he were not associated with them. I vaguely heard of Purcell's untimely death and Bradenhorst's stomach ailment for which Kingsley prescribed specialized medication. There were snippets of information disseminated that I could only partially catch.

"You are a man of faith, are you not?"

It was the first thing Kingsley said that had to do with me, but I still wasn't sure how or why.

"Yes. Enough to know I could not hold fealty to false prophets."

"This is the will of your Hebrew God. *They shall not labour in vain, nor bring forth for trouble; for they are the seed of the blessed of the Lord, and their offspring with them.* We can bring Paradise back on earth. With you as our ally, we can convince governments to bend to the greater will, the greater power."

I heard a deep voice that resonated inside me, words spoken with a profundity, with both logic and order. I could see Kingsley's mouth move but the words did not come into my ears. They were inside me.

"I can't."

"Since we drew up a compact twenty years ago, there has been no one who has remotely been able to intuit who we were and what we planned. It is almost a sign that you have come upon us. You are like Jacob wrestling with the angel. It is our duty to bless you and bring you into our fold."

The scent of sage grew stronger. The dim light of the chandelier glistened off the snifter and almost blinded me. The fingers of the otherworldly pressed against my chest and sought to enter and rip out my insides. Dick Cowan stood before me, then my mother. Rabbi Saperstein, with cold dead eyes, moved his lips but I could not hear his words. One spirit pulled at my left arm and another at my right, yet I did not move.

Finally, Kingsley's own words were jumbled, pieces of sentences missing, incomplete and incoherent thoughts.

"Bradenhorst…the stomach…gave away too much. Needed further encouragement…eliminated. Alemagna tested…Johnson…the bank. Blanc created a new…uses Devil's Breath. Along with hypnosis…You will join us. One way or another."

It took every bit of my remaining strength to stand, an act one does routinely but turned out to be nearly impossible at this moment. I turned and looked over my shoulder and heard the snake hiss somewhere along the fireplace.

Kingsley did not move. His face drooped as though he were the one exhausted from some laborious tasks. His hand swirled the snifter. The light reflected into and out of it.

I knew I had to try to leave but I could not move my feet.

"You need to sit down, Mr. Bergman." Kingsley used his doctor's voice, the kind that offered reassurance.

To me, it was the voice of the serpent. I knew not to bite into the apple.

All at once, it was as though I were in London.

The fog rolled in through the windows.

My eyes grew heavier.

Dr. Douglas Price Kingsley was no longer in the room.

He vanished without having moved a muscle or said his goodbyes.

The fog was too thick to see, to move, to breathe.

Then, there was blackness.

Chapter Twenty-Seven

For all I knew, it could have been Betty Grable who stood over me. A small light poked into one of my eyes, then the other. A stubby finger tugged on each of my lower lids to open them fully one at a time. A flat hand rested on my forehead. It felt comforting. Then the tips of two fingers on each hand checked glands in my neck. Eventually, my eyes cleared, and I continued to watch Dr. Enders examine me after a fashion. His presence did not surprise me. Rather, I was grateful to realize I was alive.

"What day?" My throat was dry, lips parched, as though I were in North Africa fighting Rommel's 7th Panzer Division. I heard a feeble whisper and hardly recognized it as my own.

"Tuesday," the doctor replied.

The last memory in my brain was a meeting with Dr. Kingsley on Saturday night. Beyond a drive in North Riverside, I had no further recollection. I could still do math, however. Three days passed. Three lost days.

Dr. Enders held me up by the back and gave me a glass of water with a straw. I started to drink like a camel, but he slowed me down and let me lay back.

"How'd I get here?"

"Some young Asian women found you in the back of the Pan American Café early Sunday morning. King Mar drove you here himself."

I did the best I could to put a smile on my face. The blessings of friendship.

I breathed in and out slowly. I couldn't function as well physically but my mind started to rejuvenate itself. I caught snippets of images and tried to recreate the lost time. It seemed like a jigsaw puzzle.

"Scopolamine?" I couldn't be sure if I spoke properly or could even be understood. The look on his face made me aware he comprehended me.

"I can't be sure. You'll have to ask her."

He stepped to his left which gave me an unobstructed view of the rest of the private room all the way to the door. A shadowy figure started to come into view. She wore the same gray suit as when I first saw her at Alan Isbell's gathering in his home. This time, the top buttons of her suit were open, and she revealed more bosom than before. Truth be told, I never expected to see FBI agent Dorothy Martin again.

It started to make sense, however, when I realized the men I chased could be deemed a threat to national security when one considered their global aspirations. Just like this past summer, I had to wonder if I played the rabbit once again.

"Could we have a moment, doctor?" Her question was not impolite but it was authoritative.

As Dr. Enders left, I caught a glimpse of a man in a suit who stood just outside the door. Dorothy Martin's look was not quite maternal nor off-putting.

"We secured the summation you composed from your librarian friend. Very concise and detailed. Showed remarkable investigatory skills. I underestimated you. Then and now."

"So, how much are you going to give me this time?"

My attempt at humor was based on the so-called reward given to me and Max Burke to basically keep quiet about the attempt to assassinate General Carl Spaatz at Lawrence Stadium this past Fourth of July.

"Perhaps you are not aware, Mr. Bergman, that, under 18 United State Code, Section 873, both blackmail and extortion are federal offenses that carry up to one year in federal prison, a substantial fine, or both." She was as serious as she needed to be.

"Skip it. I'm happy to be alive."

"And lucky." The weight of her seriousness was mitigated by a warmer tone than I heard from her previously.

"Oh?"

"We arrested Christophe Blanc. His basement contained what amounted to a laboratory. There were several restricted chemical solutions that non-military persons are forbidden to possess. We did an analysis on one beaker alone. It contained a hyoscine-based formula which we have yet to determine its practical use."

"I can probably tell you."

"I thought you could."

As best I could through a clouded mind and scratchy voice, I described my two encounters with Dr. Kingsley at his home. The first time, with limited exposure, the impact was substantial but not incapacitating. This last time was like getting hit fully in the face by Joe Louis.

Dorothy Martin continued to explain what she could. She gave all the good news before she dropped the bombshell.

"We also arrested Damiano Alemagna. He was in possession of blueprints and schematics for a wide variety of federal office buildings, bridges and tunnels, as well as the ports in Galveston and Seattle. While Blanc and Alemagna weren't caught directly in the act of sabotage, we've been working with the International Criminal Police Commission. Those folks have greater records than we can obtain."

"Kingsley?"

She sighed before she even began to speak.

"We picked him late on Sunday and questioned him through midday yesterday. Despite your analysis and theories, we couldn't connect the good doctor to any viable criminal conspiracy. His association with Wilhelm Bradenhorst was of a professional nature as his medical consultant."

"Ha!"

"We have found a prescription for *tinctura opii camphorate*. Paregoric. Apparently, Bradenhorst had stomach issues."

"I'll bet he did."

"Kingsley also had a valid explanation for his visit to Blanc."

"Oh? What was that?"

"He was returning a rare copy of *The Medical Repository* printed in 1830. We found it in Blanc's library."

"How did they meet?"

"We can't be certain. Perhaps the ICPC knows. As for Alemagna, we have found no verifiable connection to Kingsley."

I was breathless, as though I went through a full pack drill in boot camp. The lingering effects of what was likely Blanc's special formula.

"Where is he now?"

"We had to let him go." She saw my impatience, or

maybe it was my impertinence. "We've got him under surveillance." The tone was supposed to be reassuring. It didn't help. I lost faith in anyone being able to stop these men.

I was promised a five-course dinner, and all I got was an appetizer. Of the five men who founded a secret society intent upon some kind of unspecified world domination, two were dead and two had been arrested. What was presented to me was the notion they would not go free or wiggle their way out of the international justice system through some technicality. Perhaps the FBI and the ICPC had a better handle on these matters than I could consider but I had been through too much, in truth put myself through it all, for the sake of justice and righteousness.

She patted my arm and left. She told me she would visit again before she went to Washington in the next week or ten days. That would give me the time to get on my feet and think clearer.

Dr. Enders returned. He looked through a file of what I could only presume was my chart. He read carefully and had a look of dismay.

"Can you recall anything of the evening, Harold?"

"Not much. Images of his parlor. A few words. Why?"

"Mrs. Martin provided the hospital with sufficient information regarding the solution that apparently had been synthesized into a gaseous form. While it did not have the same aspects as hyoscine by itself, my review of its components indicate it could be used for inducing a hypnotic state. To what purpose I can't tell."

"I don't get it."

"You mentioned you went to Dr. Kingsley's house

on Saturday evening at seven. The reports are you were found behind the Pan American Café shortly before seven the following morning, There were no bodily injuries of any sort. Twelve hours under the influence of this concoction and you were simply released? I can't fathom it."

The insinuation here was some kind of Coué method to induce a suggestion of some kind. If that were true, I was like a wound-up alarm clock that could go off at any time. That bothered me.

I rested for the remainder of the morning and well into the afternoon. A nurse came in to check my temperature and pulse, and recorded this in my chart. A minor commotion outside my door in the late afternoon revealed I had a visitor: Eileen.

My eyes focused on her like Adam's when he awoke from his deep sleep and saw Eve for the first time. This woman who had long been a part of my life in one fashion or another appeared as though I saw her for the first time. Unfortunately, the first words out of my mouth were not indicative of warmth or tenderness.

"The cats!" The words were ejected like cartridges from a long-range weapon. To her credit, Eileen smiled warmly.

"I visited them while you've been here. They actually took to me like a mama cat."

That was all she needed to say to both reassure me and remind me of a failed attempt at declaring my love back in July. My condition would cause me to wait further.

"Thursday."

"Yes?" Her uncertainty at my comment was based on my feeble attempt to communicate.

"Rosh Hashanah. We have to go to shul."

Eileen's face was a mix of surprise, satisfaction, and uncertainty. Here it was Tuesday. I had gone through what felt like a mustard gas attack. All I could consider was the High Holidays.

At that moment, Dr. Enders returned. Eileen now had an outlet to assist me. She started simply with an inquiry about my prognosis followed by what sounded like a request to attend temple services.

"Well, that's what I was coming to tell you. All your tests have come back clean. While you are suffering fatigue from this incident, there should be nothing to stop you from going to temple. The release papers will be finalized in about fifteen minutes or so."

Charlie Argento and his hack waited patiently outside. I walked normally but was strained by the effort. With the exception of going to temple, I had no plans for the foreseeable future.

Eileen indicated my car was found a half mile from Kingsley's home. The police towed it to my apartment after they completed their investigation. She responded only to my questions and just allowed me to return to whatever it was I called normal.

Lady Mittens and Sir Pounce stood about five feet away from me as I walked in, both mewing loud enough to drown out fireworks on the Fourth of July. I imagined they were upset at my absence and castigated me for the possibility they would have been orphaned yet again. I slowly kneeled and extended a hand to each. The silence returned and two sets of ears got rubbed.

"There is bread and eggs and coffee and milk," Eileen declared motherly. "I don't know what you eat on a regular basis. So—"

I grabbed her hands, pulled her toward me, and kissed her as strongly and passionately as I ever had in my life. I wrapped my arms around her and held on as though she were the only thing that could keep me alive. Perhaps she was.

"We need to talk." I heard myself sound far too serious.

"Yes, but not now. You need to rest. I'll come by tomorrow." She started to leave, then turned suddenly. "I think you need to contact Ma Bell about getting a phone in here. This private detective business of yours is really starting to take off."

When she left, I felt like a little kid who was told he could have his cake and eat it, too. Eileen was worried about me but at the same time understood that I had the strength and resilience to get through a lot, certainly more than either of us could have imagined. Then I remembered four years of violent warfare and understood how strong I could be. As for her, she would always worry about me because that is what you do when you love someone. I now had no doubt of her feelings.

Yet even though I possessed the courage to make a life with her, the comment by Dr. Enders was disconcerting:

You mentioned you went to Dr. Kingsley's house on Saturday evening at seven. The reports are you were found behind the Pan American Café shortly before seven the following morning, There were no bodily injuries of any sort. Twelve hours under the influence of this concoction and you were simply released? I can't fathom it.

There was much to be concerned about, yet I did not allow it to stop me in my tracks and keep me from pursuing the life I led. I knew I was guided by faith, that Adonai would guide me and keep me on the right path. As was said in Isaiah 30:21 – *And thine ears shall hear a word behind thee, saying, This is the way, walk ye in it, when ye turn to the right hand, and when ye turn to the left.*

All I had to do was listen.

Chapter Twenty-Eight

Two pairs of feline eyes gazed upon me as I woke. I wanted to believe they simply wished to look out for me. Then it dawned on me they couldn't do it on an empty stomach. They split a can of their food while I boiled a couple of eggs and made coffee. I was hungry but wasn't sure what I could take.

It was a foolish notion to revisit the so-called scene of the crime, but I needed to come to some understanding of what Kingsley was really all about. It was also rather imprudent of me to attempt to drive but I knew I needed to face the demons and move on.

To my surprise, the front gate was open. When I drove in, I parked next to a gray Nash which I recalled only too well from this past summer. I couldn't imagine why Dorothy Martin would be there. The front door was ajar as though I were expected.

I found her kneeling by the fireplace near where I sat on the two occasions of my prior visits. I let her continue whatever she did while I perused the room in a more clear-headed fashion. The coat of arms with the Latin quote looked less ominous.

Dorothy Martin stood, brushed off her hands, and walked across to the chair where Dr. Kingsley sat. She reached along the arms until she found what she looked for.

"There's a pipe neatly tucked into the brick there. It goes to a tank of some sort in the basement which is currently empty. Over here," she said, pointing to the arm of the chair, "is a button which likely activates a release of the gas. We are still having it analyzed."

"Isn't that enough to arrest Kingsley?" I thought I knew how the law worked given my background and experience. I acted like a rookie all over again.

"Circumstantial. It could be claimed the tank contained a cleansing vaporized solution to enhance air quality. Blanc had the chemicals and Alemagna had the blueprints. That is cold evidence. I'll bet a nickel Kingsley led this group and knew exactly what he was doing."

"Well, it's a good thing you have him under surveillance."

Her head dipped. I guessed it wasn't her shoes she looked at. I was suddenly grateful for the light breakfast as I assumed I was about to get sick.

"We followed him to Union Station, watched him buy a ticket and board, then got on to find him. He wasn't there."

"So, he doubled back and got off and now you have no idea where he is." I did not comment as a question because it was obvious. I wasn't concerned for my own well-being. Knowing who this man was and what he was capable of had me scared for the rest of the world.

"We'll find him."

"I doubt it."

I turned sharply and left. To her credit, she didn't follow me and engage in a series of melodramatic promises. In my mind, there were many bad and evil people in the world wanting to do harm to others. Dr.

Douglas Price Kingsley was just one of them. He could stand in line with the rest of them.

My friend, confidante, and now benefactor, King Mar, gave me a hug that any Jewish grandmother would have envied. He even pinched my cheeks to reassure himself of my good health.

"I can't lose my best customer." His eyes glazed a bit but he held back the tears. He and a waitress came in early this past Sunday morning to prepare the menu for the day and set the tables. They found me leaning upright to the side of the back door. At first, the waitress took me for a bum sleeping one off, but King Mar recognized me immediately. I was somewhere between unconscious and delirious. He drove me to Wesley Medical Center, rambling in Chinese until nurses put me on a gurney and brought me into an examination room. The emergency room doctor came about an hour later to indicate I was alive and stabilized. Dr. Enders consulted with King Mar and asked him to notify my family and anyone of consequence.

As he recited this unique adventure, I couldn't help but appreciate how blessed I was. Obviously, I found favor in the eyes of the Lord.

My father almost immediately castigated me for driving before he hugged me seemingly with a notion to never let me go. He held my face in his hands, shook his head, then started to cry. It was his desire to possess little of this world. A comfortable home and a family were all he deemed necessary. After the loss of his wife, my mother, the thought of losing me likely devasted him. He knew, as did I, that Hezekiah was on his deathbed and prayed fervently for which the Lord granted him fifteen more years. We are allowed to make our own future.

Such is our faith.

I went to Farmers and Bankers Life Insurance and waited patiently to visit with Troy Harding. He welcomed me like a long-lost cousin, shook my hand passionately, and graciously offered me a seat.

"So, you're doing okay?" he asked considerately.

"As well as can be expected."

"Is Mr. Johnson safe?"

"I believe so." Without going into too much detail, I gave him an idea of what this group planned to do. In my estimation, William Johnson was a test case to verify they had the means to control men's minds. There would likely be no further repercussions.

Troy Harding pulled a check from his desk drawer and slid it across the desk. It was made out to me in the amount of five thousand dollars.

"This is from Mr. Johnson and, well, us here at Farmers and Bankers."

"I can't take this, Mr. Harding."

To a man for whom money is the primary motivation in life, he appeared perplexed. This sum represented more money than half the population made in a year. Given my simplistic lifestyle, this could have held me over for many years. What Troy Harding couldn't understand was this money could not heal my limp or erase the memories of bitter warfare and the loss of so many friends and comrades. Any amount wouldn't help my grieving over Caroline Whitman and Dale Walker or guide a young girl like Debra Rose Nathan who had already seen more before she was twenty than most see in their entire lives.

He said he understood. I believed him. I told him the position he created for me was no longer tenable and that

I could not work efficiently within the confines of a corporate system. He shook my hand as a gentleman and suppressed whatever disappointment he might have experienced. The noble experiment ended.

For the remainder of that day, I drank coffee and took stock of my life. I truly felt charged to aid the many good people that I encountered, and knew they would be interspersed with the unholy and the evil. I had the education, the willpower, and the means to put to right the wrongs of those who needed a guardian angel, so to speak. My own desires and wishes would need to be secondary.

Eileen got off early from work the next night so that we could attend the first night of Rosh Hashanah services after sundown. We picked up my father and walked in together. Many people were gratified to see me, both in terms of my absence over the years as well as those who were aware of my recent plight. All told, it was more like a homecoming.

Rabbi Saperstein, now nearly blind, sat on the bema and nodded as Rabbi Mendel conducted the service. This night marked the beginning of the Days of Awe, ten nights of penitence, ten nights to reflect on the prior year. It was right about then I ventured into the world of the private detective and was able to get a former councilman's daughter away from an ex-bootlegger. I had been to the darkest parts of the city where I found people with good hearts as well as opulent homes that harbored the immoral. I was accepted by those with whom I had nothing in common. I bonded with all who carried goodness in their heart.

My father and Eileen were both captivated by the proceedings. I looked around in astonishment at how easily I felt comfortable here. It was like Jack Robin returned to temple to perform the Kol Nidre as Jakie Rabinowitz. I made too much of it, overthought it. In reflection, I really never left.

We drove my father home. He surprised me by not inviting us inside. Perhaps the day's activities and my return from what seemed like the dead tired him out. He might also have recognized it was more important for me to spend time with Eileen.

We took a booth at Candyland. She ordered a malted and a Danish. I drank coffee with my apple pie. We simply sat and looked at each other. I wondered which one of us would break the spell first.

"You know," she said right as I uttered "I was thinking" and we both laughed.

"I'm so proud of you," she said. She actually started to tear up. "You are smarter, stronger, and more generous than I could ever imagine. I am so grateful you are alive, I don't care about nothing else. I would sit with you in Candyland over pie and Danish for the rest of my life if that was all I could have."

I reached across the table and held both of her hands in mine. I heard a statement of love blended with what sounded like sacrifice, that her happiness was bound only to my living and that she didn't need to be a part of it. I could not accept that.

"You silly girl. Here I was trying to figure out if you would be comfortable in my apartment with Lady Mittens and Sir Pounce." She looked at me in shock. "We had a picnic in the park back in July that was interrupted. Do you remember?"

"I do."

I let her hands go, sat back, and folded my arms

across my chest.

"Would you be willing to repeat those words in temple?"

Her mouth fell open. She didn't move a muscle, didn't blink an eye, didn't utter a sound. Perhaps I had the ability to hypnotize.

"I don't want you to change. I don't want you to stop being a private detective or give up this journey, this mission you are on."

"But I will have to change. Someday. I wasn't always a soldier. I wasn't always a police officer. I became those as part of a path in life. I don't know where it leads. But it doesn't matter. As long as you are with me, we honor Adonai, we honor our family—"

"And we honor each other."

I wanted to do more than ask. I wanted to say something profound. Instead, I found myself tongue-tied like Moses.

"Will you marry me?"

No sooner had I blurted out the words did I realize what men are supposed to do in these occasions: offer a ring as a token of intention, perhaps even get on one knee and formally propose. It didn't seem to matter.

The seeds of love that were planted in our youth were now fully blossomed.

A word about the author…

I studied film-making and creative writing at the University of Miami in the 80's, was involved in the Boston Poetry Scene in the 90's, and am a former president of the Kansas Writer's Association. My work has stretched from crime fiction to poetry, screen writing to experimental fiction. I am also co-host of Tikiman and The Viking podcast

(https://open.spotify.com/show/5R3wY5THZtBGI08JX7yJn7#_=_)

I live in Wichita, KS with my wife, Shelia, and Sir Pounce Alot (the orange manx) and Lady Mittens (the tuxedo manx).

BLOG: http://tikiman1962.wordpress.com

http://tikiman1962.wordpress.com

Thank you for purchasing
this publication of The Wild Rose Press, Inc.

For questions or more information
contact us at
info@thewildrosepress.com.

The Wild Rose Press, Inc.
www.thewildrosepress.com

www.ingramcontent.com/pod-product-compliance
Lightning Source LLC
Chambersburg PA
CBHW070107030726
47506CB00002B/622
* 9 7 8 1 5 0 9 2 6 3 4 1 7 *